THE KRINAR EXPERIMENT

A KRINAR WORLD NOVEL

CHARMAINE PAULS

Published by Charmaine Pauls

Montpellier, 34090, France

www.charmainepauls.com

Published in France

Cover design by Najla Qamber Designs

(www.najlaqamberdesigns.com)

ISBN: 978-2-9561031-2-7 (eBook)

ISBN: 978-1-7233608-6-2 (Print)

❀ Created with Vellum

1

"**C**ode red!"

Drako overrode the autopilot and seized the throttle as the pod continued to lose altitude. No matter how hard he pushed up, the nose of the craft continued to dive down.

"Crute," he muttered under his breath. "Control, fix it. Now!"

A static noise crackled over the communication system, followed by the voice of Commander Ruwan in Krina. "Your pod doesn't respond. It seems to be a problem with the Earth's atmospheric qualities."

Red lights lit up the control panel, every one of them blaring at him.

"I'm going down."

Ruwan's command was calm and controlled. "Abandon the pod."

"I've lost my invisibility." He didn't have to elaborate. If he crashed on Earth, Earthlings would discover the pod. The reconnaissance mission was top secret. The Krinar's existence wasn't meant to be known. At least, not yet. "I can try to land and fix the problem."

"Abandon the pod," Ruwan repeated, this time with a stronger tone.

Drako applied more pressure to the throttle, managing to slow down his descent a fraction. The skyline of Johannesburg, South Africa's so called City of Gold, became visible. The pod started shaking, clattering his bones in his chair.

"Drako," Ruwan said, "eject yourself from the craft, or I'll do it for you."

Drako gnashed his teeth. He couldn't disobey a direct command.

"Abandoning ship," he conceded. "On three."

"We're following your coordinates. A rescue mission is on the way."

"One, two..." Drako dragged in a breath. Damn. He hated jettisoning. "Three!"

He slammed his palm down on the touch button that would enclose him in a capsule and deposit him on the planet he was supposed to spy on. The homing signal on the capsule would give Krina his coordinates.

Nothing.

Zut!

"It's not working!" he exclaimed unnecessarily. The technical team in Krina had a visual via their comms system.

The controls went haywire. The smoky pollution drifting atop the skyscrapers and mine dumps was dangerously close. There was only one option left.

"Emergency landing!"

"Do not--"

Ruwan's voice cut at the same time as the communication panel went dead. Damnation. This was bad. He was stuck in a faulty pod, no longer concealed from sight to the inhabitants of a planet who were ignorant about the Krinar's existence, going down into one of the most dangerous cities of this world, and all electronic functions were dead. So was his palm device. The last coordinates the pod had sent to the control tower in Krina had been several space miles back. He was effectively visible to the Earth people and invisible to his own.

He thanked the stars for his interest in antiques. If not for that passion, he'd never have learned how to manipulate flying crafts manually. He needed every bit of that knowledge to steer the lightweight, sleek pod through the mass of manmade constructions without crashing into one of the gloomy towers.

His heart pummeling in his ribcage, he scanned the environment. The only feasible emergency landing spot where he wouldn't endanger the lives of any of the Earth species was an arena. His brain did a quick, automatic reference check, filtering through the intelligence he'd studied. Humans referred to it as a sports stadium. He swerved east and tilted thirty degrees, even if his approach was too fast for a landing. This was his only shot. If he missed the field, he'd crash into one of the buildings beyond.

Clutching the throttle between both hands, he pushed down and stepped on the pedals to release the emergency landing wings. If too soon, they'd be ripped off by the force of his speed. Once the wings were safely extended, he applied the flap breaks. Earth dwellings stacked high upon each other--apartment buildings-- whizzed past him, blurring in his sight. Three more seconds. The oblong shape of the arena grew in size. Aiming for the green vegetation in the middle, he braced himself.

The pod collided with the planet with a force Drako couldn't physically foresee despite his intellectual knowledge of Earth's gravity. The impact threw his body forward. He protected his face with his arms as he slammed into the controls. His body rattled from the shock. The only thing that prevented him from being crushed was the safety harness. The intelligent material that constituted the pod didn't adapt or give. In this strange airspace with its grave atmospheric qualities, the usually moldable substance remained a hard surface with sharp metal fixtures and combustible gas. However, he was still breathing. Miraculously, so.

Pain lanced at Drako from all sides. The sensation was foreign to him. He stared at his body in surprise. The skin flayed on his shoulder, revealing tendons and bone underneath. Blood trickled from his side. A long gash burned on his shin. The control panel had broken in two, the ridges that pushed up sporting bits of skin. That explained the injuries. Carefully, he rotated his neck and shook his limbs. Except for a few bruised ribs, his other bones seemed to be intact. Extremely fortunate. At the moment, his greatest health risk was the blood loss. Making quick work of it, he unclipped the harness and freed himself. The first aid kit with the nano-healer was stored with the nutrients behind the pilot's seat.

He didn't manage to turn before a small explosion on the side of the fuel pocket rocked the pod, ripping a hole in the panel and flinging his body through it. The heat was excruciating, but his fire-resistant pilot jumper suit absorbed most of it and enabled him to put out the flames by rolling on the prickly, green soil before the fabric had completely disintegrated.

Lying naked on the grass, he hardly registered the pain any longer as one, encompassing thought consumed his mind. Put out the fire. If the pod exploded, not only would he have no means of returning home, but the nano-healer would also be gone. He'd be as good as dead. Fighting dizziness––another novel experience–– he dragged his upper body forward by his arms. His legs refused to obey his brain's command to get up and walk. The nanocytes in his body that should've aided in his quick healing had to have been damaged in the crash. In another few meters, the blackness became a bigger threat than the flames. If he lost consciousness, all was doomed. He tried to drag himself around to the other side where he could grab hold of the fire extinguisher when he caught a blur of movement in his peripheral vision. Jerking his face in that direction, he assessed the visual input. A bunch of humans were storming toward him.

Zut. He didn't need this intervention. A new burst of

adrenaline allowed his mind to overrule his nervous system. Pushing to his feet, he took a wide stance in front of his craft. The threat of his body language was clear. Even if he'd mastered Earth language in all of its dialects, he didn't need words to get this message across. The humans slowed, and then paused. For five stifling heartbeats they measured each other, and then the bravest of the pack broke free. The human charged like a rabid dog, tattered clothes flapping around him. Expecting a full-blown attack, Drako was surprised when the human jerked off his patched jacket in the run and started pounding the flames. The rest of the pack followed suit. Arms flailing and clothes waving, they effectively put out the fire.

Maybe there was a way out of this without causing global pandemonium. Maybe he could say he was testing a new secret plane and pay off the witnesses to keep their mouths shut. Judging by the state of their garments, they looked like they could do with the bribe. First, he needed to get that first-aid kit. He took a step toward the smoldering pod, but wobbled on his feet. He had to be losing blood faster than he'd thought, or maybe it was a concussion.

The circle of humans opened when he neared unsteadily, their eyes trained on him warily.

"Thank you," he said, practicing the smile that was the non-verbal sign for a friendly greeting.

As he held out a hand, as per the Earth custom, his body finally failed him, giving over to the darkest threat of all–– unconsciousness––but not before he'd spotted the helicopter with the South African Secret Service emblem lifting above the buildings and noise.

2

The waiting area of the Johannesburg General Hospital was swamped. So were the corridors and every other passage. Patients spilled out from everywhere, overflowing a health system that already had its back breaking under a too great a demand and too little resources.

Nurse Ilse Gouws finished bandaging a stab wound and stretched her back. Wiping a hand over her brow, she stared through the open window at the summer day. The sky was purple with a pending thunderstorm. The welcome smell of rain would soften the sharp odor of disinfectant.

"I hate storms," Caitlin Visage said next to her.

Ilse smiled at the matron. "At least it will cool down the air."

She waved in the next patient, a woman with tuberculosis who'd come for her monthly treatment. The lady shuffled inside and lowered herself with some difficulty into the only chair.

"We're out of Rifampin," Caitlin said, glancing over Ilse's shoulder at the clipboard.

"How can we be out of Rifampin? I signed off the batch we received on Monday myself."

"It was stolen."

"Again?" Ilse propped her hands on her hips, feeling the helplessness to her bones. "What are we doing to catch the culprits?"

"The police said they couldn't do anything. They don't have time to investigate our stolen medicine while there are more severe cases to solve."

"I can't believe it. We must be able to do *something?*"

"Like what? I've changed the locks God only knows how many times."

"Clearly, it's an inside job. We could paint the next batches with invisible ink and scan the hands of every staff member who works on this floor."

"That's discriminatory. By law, we're not allowed to plant traps for our employees. Wouldn't hold up in court." Caitlin gave a half-mast smile. "I've already mentioned that idea to the last constable who took my statement."

Ilse blew out a drawn-out breath. Complaining wasn't going to help the patient staring at her with expectant eyes. She searched the form on her clipboard for the woman's name. Mosa Nzama.

Pursing her lips, she crouched down in front of the woman with the wrinkled dress and skin. "How long have you been waiting, Mosa?"

"Four hours, Miss."

Her heart ached with compassion. "We're out of stock, right now. Why don't you give me your address, and when the new stock comes in, I'll deliver it personally."

"Ilse." Caitlin's hand fell soft on her shoulder. "We don't know *if* a new batch will come in."

Ilse ignored the matron. "How about that?" She gave Mosa's hand a reassuring pat, a poor consolation for the medicine she deserved.

"That's very kind of you," Mosa said. "Would you really do that?"

"How long did it take you to get here?"

"Hours. There was a long wait at the taxi rank, and I walked some of the way."

"Here." Ilse took a notepad from the desk and handed it to her with a pen. "Write down your address and your number, and I'll call you before I come over."

Mosa averted her eyes. "I don't have a number."

"Never mind. Just your address will do."

As Mosa started scribbling, Caitlin gave Ilse a reprimanding look, but the matron only verbally objected again when the patient was gone.

"You can't do that for everyone," Caitlin argued. "Plus, you don't know where she lives." She stared after the woman's disappearing form. "It may not be safe for you to go there."

"At least I'll make a difference to one life," she said, dismissing the subject by immersing herself in preparing the examination bed for the next patient.

"Your shift's been over a long time," Caitlin said. "Go home and sleep. You're no good to me dead on your feet."

Ilse glanced at the clock. It was almost five in the afternoon. True, she'd been on duty since four that morning, and she felt the hours in every fiber of her being. "In a minute. I'll finish cleaning up in here, and then I'll go."

"Matron Visage?" a voice said from the door.

The women turned in unison.

A bulky man stood in the frame. He was dressed in civilian clothes, but a pistol holster showed from under his jacket. He held a badge to the matron. "Agent Pillay. I need a nurse to come with me. We have a prisoner with substantial injuries who needs treatment."

Strands of hair flew from Caitlin's bun as she shook her head. "You'll have to speak to a doctor."

The man put the badge away and hooked a thumb into his belt. "I already did. They're understaffed."

"So are we."

"Ms. Visage, I'm here on government order. Don't make me use force."

"It's Matron to you," she said with a lift of her nose. "Where is this patient?"

"In safe holding," he answered.

"Where would that happen to be?"

"Downtown."

She pointed a finger at the line of waiting patients. "See for yourself what we're dealing with. I don't have time to send a nurse downtown to tend to your prisoner. Bring him here if he needs treatment."

His cheekbones darkened. "*Matron*, you don't want to push me on this."

"I'll go," Ilse said quickly. "My shift has ended, anyway."

Caitlin turned sharp eyes on her. "You've worked twelve hours straight. I need you fresh back here in eight. What you need is a shower, a meal, and to sleep, not to gallivant downtown on a Mother Teresa mission."

The agent looked Ilse up and down. "What kind of experience do you have?"

"I work *here*. What do you think?" Ilse challenged.

He nodded once. "You'll do. Follow me."

As he turned and she scurried to follow, Caitlin caught her arm. "You're wearing yourself out."

"Don't worry. It's just going down to the prison and applying a Band-aid or two. I'll be home, showered, and sleeping before you know it. Happy?"

Caitlin exhaled on a puff.

"Good." Ilse winked. "See you tomorrow."

The agent was waiting for her in the corridor, tapping his foot. "I don't have all day, Nurse…"

"Gouws. Let me grab my bag and a medical kit, and I'll be right with you."

9

"You don't need a medical kit. We've got everything covered."

"Oh." She'd been on prison call-out twice, and in both instances she'd taken all the medical supplies. She didn't have time to ponder the issue, because Agent Pillay was already making his way down the hallway in long strides.

THIRSTY. His body needed rehydration. Drako forced open his eyes. They burned. The air on this planet, at least where he was now, was filthy. A recollection of the crash rammed into his conscience. His whole body jerked. The pain was still there, only worse, but there was something else, too. He tried to move his arms and legs. His suspicion was confirmed. He was tied up. He turned his head an inch. If not for the situation, he would've laughed at the ropes that secured his wrists and ankles to four bedposts. For now, he didn't break them. He scanned his surroundings, preferring to analyze the danger first.

He was lying on what humans would refer to as a mattress, which was suspended on a bed. According to the smell, it was unclean. Lumpy. A very uncomfortable invention. It was soaked red with his blood. The walls of the chamber were white, but stained. The floor was no better, the tiles chipped and in need of degerming. He was alone by appearance, only. The red light in the corner of the ceiling suggested company.

True to his expectations, it didn't take the Earthlings long after he'd opened his eyes to make their appearance. A metal door opened, and three men stepped inside. They all wore the same uniform. The logo on their shirts stated SASS. South African Secret Service. His worst nightmare come true.

Even with all three men armed with pistols, they kept their distance.

The oldest of the men took a step forward. "Do you speak our language?"

Drako chuckled. "Of course, I do."

The men stared at him, open-mouthed.

"What are you?" the one in the middle asked.

How gullible would they be? "A test pilot from Denel." He'd studied their organizations beforehand, knowing Denel fabricated their military aircrafts.

Two of the men exchanged a look. It was the third who replied. "Denel hasn't been operational for fifteen years."

"Not that you know of."

The man who'd spoken first walked to the far wall and removed a hose. He approached the foot end of the bed. "There are ways of making you talk."

Drako strained his neck to watch the man. "Where is my plane?" He said *plane* carefully, just like he'd memorized. "The testing is classified."

"It's in a safe place. In time, we'll take you there," he grinned, "and you'll show us how it works, as our technicians can't figure it out. Yet."

Drako's muscles tensed so much he almost snapped the ropes. "If you touched it…"

"Of course we have," the man said. "Now, let's start again. What are you?" As he asked the question, he pushed the hose to the sole of Drako's foot. An electric current zapped through Drako's body. His muscles pulled tight, held in a painful vice from electricity. When the man finally let up, Drako was panting. His jaw ached from the tension.

Seriously? They used *shock therapy*? Exactly how backward were they?

"Well?" the man asked with a smug expression on his ugly Earthly face.

Drako uttered a throaty laugh. "All right. Thanks for making the rules clear."

"Turn it up," the man said to his colleagues.

One of the men approached an antique looking device on a

gurney and manipulated a dial switch. He'd scarcely finished when his accomplice zapped Drako again. His body arched off the mattress, his fingers and toes curling with painful spasms. It felt as if his insides were being ripped apart. A few more volts and his brain would be fried.

"Talk!" the man said, aiming the hose at Drako's exposed genitals.

Enough.

A roar tore from his chest. He flexed his arms and legs. It didn't take more than that to snap the ropes. In a millisecond, he was on his feet. His baffled attacker dropped the hose, scurrying for a corner while the other two drew their weapons. Before any shots could be fired, Drako grabbed their wrists and pointed the weapons away from him. A crack sounded, followed by a chilling scream. One of the guns fell to the floor. Drako stared at the arm in his grip. The hand hung limp. Crute, these Earthlings were fragile. He'd popped the man's wrist without any thought of applying such damaging pressure. He was still assessing the surprising damage when the man in the corner raised his gun. Drako ducked before the shot went off, swinging the second armed guard he still held by the arm around as a shield to discourage the other from firing his bullets, but the weight suddenly disappeared from his grasp. Another bloodcurdling cry filled the space. In his hand, he held nothing but an arm. Zut. Were these men made of cardboard? Drako gawked at the flesh in his hand. The man whose limb he'd severed was thankfully unconscious. The remaining two stared at him, their fear a sulfurous smell even stronger than that of the coppery blood.

"Kill him," the man with the broken wrist screamed.

The one in the corner was still aiming his gun, but the weapon shook too much in his grip to take a clear shot.

"Stop," Drako said. "I don't want to hurt you." *More,* he added in his mind with a regretful sigh.

"What the fuck are you?" the man with the gun shouted hysterically.

His cover was blown. There was no point in pretending he was testing a secret plane any longer. As for being human, he'd never pass as one. Not after today.

"Take me to my pod." He nodded at the unconscious man who was losing blood even faster than himself. "I can heal him."

"Don't listen to him! Shoot him! Shoot the motherfucker before he kills us with his bare hands."

Before Drako could deliver a more convincing argument assuring them he meant no harm, the door opened and several men in similar uniforms armed with automatic rifles rushed through.

Drako lifted his hands, palms facing forward, in the Earthlings' non-verbal command for cease-fire. "Take me to my pod, and all will be well for everyone."

"Like hell," a man with red hair and a bushy moustache mumbled. "Stick him."

The muscle of Drako's upper arm twitched as something sharp pierced the skin. A hypodermic needle stuck out from his arm. He pulled the injector from his flesh. The odor was sharp on his enhanced olfactory sense, but one he was unfamiliar with. Surrounded by SS guards, it was hard to say where the assault had come from, not that it mattered. There were too many of them. He was about to launch into another speech, appealing to their common senses to let him heal the wounds he'd sustained and those he'd inflicted when Earth tipped under his feet and gravity spun out of control.

3

The downpour started in all earnest before Ilse and Agent Pillay had made it to his car in the outside parking lot. If she hadn't been running late this morning, she would've taken her umbrella. There had been no forecast for rain, but summer thunderstorms were always unpredictable, arriving almost daily around four in the afternoon and clearing up an hour later to leave the earth with a smell as enticing as clean laundry and a pretty rainbow to make up for the boisterous thunder and explosive lightning.

Holding her bag over her head, Ilse lengthened her steps to keep up with Agent Pillay. The wind whipped the rain against her face, the drops stinging her cheeks. Her tunic and shoes were soaked by the time the agent had unlocked the door to let her in. Before closing the door, she squeezed the water from her braid in a futile attempt to not spoil his leather seats.

"Sorry about that," he mumbled as he got in beside her.

She offered him a friendly smile. "It's not your fault. You can't control the weather."

"I meant not having an umbrella."

"That's all right. I forgot mine, too."

She shivered as he started the engine and air from the air con hit her with a blast. Thankfully, he switched it off before pulling out of the hospital parking lot. As the Nelson Mandela Bridge appeared, he pulled onto the curb. They could get fined for obstructing traffic, not to mention that it was dangerous being parked on the narrow roadside. A car could slam into them and push them through the barrier and over the side.

She sat up straighter. "Is something the matter?"

He reached inside his jacket pocket and pulled out a blindfold.

She looked between the strip of cloth and his expressionless face. "Are you kidding me?"

"Protocol."

When she didn't reach for it, his jaw tightened. "Put it on, Nurse Gouws, and make a speedy job of it."

She snatched the fabric from his hand and tied it behind her head.

"Good," he said, satisfaction bleeding into his voice.

Without making further conversation, he steered them back onto the road. She tried to keep her bearings and discern their direction, but they'd taken several turns by the time he pulled to a stop and said, "You can remove the blindfold."

They were in an underground parking. From the few cars in the lot, it wasn't a busy building. Green paint peeled from the walls, and the concrete floor was stained with car oil.

He opened his door. "Come on."

Without waiting to see if she was following, he turned for an elevator that was operated by an armed guard. The uniform was SS, not police force or correctional services. Once they were inside, the guard pressed the button for minus four, and the elevator started moving with a jolt. According to the numbers on the panel, there were eight floors above ground and four under. They exited on the lowest level. Agent Pillay led her along a hallway with a low ceiling. Tungsten lights flickered overhead.

They passed several metal doors, all fitted with deadbolts. The facility had to be old. The prison she'd visited in Pretoria had electronic locks on the cells that worked with a code. She suppressed a shiver that had nothing to do with her wet clothes. At the last door, he stopped. A group of men in civilian clothes were gathered outside.

"This is Agent Evans," Agent Pillay said, indicating a man with copper hair and a big moustache. "He'll take over." He left with a salute.

Agent Evans extended a hand. "Call me Pete."

She shook his hand. "Ilse Gouws."

"Ms. Gouws––"

"Ilse, please."

"Ilse, did Agent Pillay tell you anything about our prisoner?"

"Nothing."

He nodded his approval. "The less you know, the better, except that he's a convicted felon, a dangerous man who committed terrible crimes."

The shiver she managed to maintain until then escaped. "What kind of crimes?"

"I'm afraid I can't elaborate. All you need to concern yourself with are his injuries." He motioned to a man on his left with a casted wrist. "Agent Frik Retief is in charge of our medical supplies. He prepared everything you should need."

"What kind of injuries are we talking about?"

"You'll see," he said evasively.

Agent Retief ran his eyes over the length of her. "Ready?"

She took a breath and steeled herself. Prison fights could cause nasty injuries, and not knowing what to expect, made it worse. "Yes, Agent."

"Please, why so formal? It's Frik."

"All right, Frik. Let's see your prisoner."

Frik flicked his fingers at one of the men standing guard at the door who immediately pulled back the deadbolt.

"Ilse?" Pete touched her shoulder.

She turned back to face him. "Yes?"

"You can't speak to anyone about this man or what you did here today. This case is classified. Government business. If you mention anything about what you've seen, you'll force me to *take action*. Understand?"

The underlying threat in his words was clear.

"Of course."

"Good. You can go in now."

The door swung open, and Frik stood aside for her to enter. From the part of the room she glimpsed through the doorway, it was a concrete dungeon with a gray slab ceiling, floor, and walls. She stepped over the threshold cautiously. The temperature was too cold to be comfortable. Goosebumps broke out over her arms and legs. The inside smelled of damp, blood, and sweat. Her nostrils twitched at a faint odor of something like burnt hair.

"Go on," Frik said, waving her in impatiently.

For some reason she was hesitant to go deeper into the room. She couldn't stop another quake from crawling over her skin. Claustrophobia constricted her throat. Her palms turned clammy. This was nothing like the prison cells where she'd bandaged stab wounds. What *was* this place?

All thoughts fled her mind when she rounded the door. She stopped dead, her heart jostling in her chest. Against the far wall, a man was shackled in chains, his arms and legs spread wide, stretching him into an X. Blood dripped from his side. His shoulder was cut open to the bone, and there was a nasty gash on his shin. She had no problem in seeing his wounds, because he was stark naked.

His head hung low, hiding his face from her. The skin that wasn't smeared with blood and dirt was smooth and flawless with a golden sheen. Too flawless. If not for the corded muscles that twitched under his lean form, he could've been a wax statue or a mannequin. He was unnaturally tall. She barely reached his chest.

His short-cropped hair was a dark caramel color, thick and glossy. The rest of his body was hairless. Even his genitals. She couldn't help noticing the size of his penis. Dear God. She'd never seen anything like it, and she saw a lot of naked bodies in her profession. Thick and long, it hung heavy between his legs. Flawless, like the rest of him.

Out of respect, she drew her gaze away, not lingering to explore the intimate details of his nakedness. Indignity on his behalf evoked her compassion and anger. The least they could do was cover him. She was about to say so when he lifted his head, and their eyes connected.

A yellow gaze simmering with sparks collided with hers. She sucked in a breath. The intensity of his stare was brutal. She felt it right to her soul, to where she was a woman first and a nurse second. His nostrils flared slightly as he kept his eyes trained on her, his chest rising and falling with a deep breath. His face was strikingly perfect, a work of art. A thin, straight nose was set off against high cheekbones and a proud chin. His full lips would've been sensual had they not been pulled into a sneer. There were no words to describe him. He was a magnificent specimen. Whatever he was, he wasn't human, not with those eerie eyes, too perfect face, and too large body. He was something else.

Something different.

Something … frightening.

Despite his injuries and awkward imprisonment, his comportment was regal. He held his shoulders square and his back straight. He looked down at her from his impressive height, as a ruler would measure a subordinate. His gaze moved over her face, seeming to analyze her features to the smallest detail. The piercing stare moved down and came to a stop midway. His head tilted with the slightest angle. Unabashedly, unapologetically, he studied her breasts. Under his scrutiny, her nipples hardened. She looked down at the wet fabric of her white tunic. It had to be see-through. Her cheeks heated uncomfortably. It took all her willpower not to cover herself up with her arms. Doing so would signal that she was aware of him, and it wasn't professional behavior for a veteran nurse to see a man as anything other than a patient. His lips twitched, as if he called her bluff.

Frik's voice broke through her thoughts. "Are you going to do something or just stand there?"

The spell that held her immobile broke. She tore her gaze away from the prisoner's and jerked back to life. The man was critically injured. The fact that he was still standing was a miracle, never mind that he was standing there like a king instead of a man chained in the deepest, darkest of basements.

She turned her fury on Frik. "This man has to go to a hospital."

The agent shook his head. "Not going to happen."

"He needs a doctor."

"He's not getting one. You're his best shot."

"Prisoner or not, he's entitled to medical attention."

"Wake up and smell the roses, honey. The country is short of doctors. Right now, there's no one but you, so march your butt over there and do your job." He smirked. "We could wait it out until a state doctor becomes available, but it won't be for hours. By then, he may be dead."

The stubborn look on his face told her he wasn't going to budge. Worse, the spark of malice in his eyes indicated he might be happy if the prisoner didn't make it. Whatever the man had done to deserve such ire, it wasn't her job to judge. Her job was to cure, to save lives if it was in her power to do so. It was what she'd promised when she'd taken her oath.

She turned back to the man, gauging his wounds. The pain had to be excruciating.

She straightened her spine with resolve. "Uncuff him."

Frik looked at her like she'd lost her mind. "What?"

"Take off the chains."

He glanced at a mirror on the opposite wall. Probably a one-way mirror. They were being watched.

"I can't help him if he's chained to the wall," she said.

"You don't know what he did the last time his hands were free." He lifted his casted wrist. *"This* is nothing compared to the other things he did."

She swallowed away the dryness in her throat. "Release him and give him a bed to lie down on."

Frik took two threatening steps toward her. "He ripped a man's arm straight off." He flicked his fingers. "Just like that. Saw it with my own eyes."

Pete walked into the room. He gave Frik a look, wordlessly communicating something she didn't understand.

"Fine." Frik took a key from his pocket and threw it at her feet. "Have it your way."

"We don't have a bed on site," Pete said. "You'll have to make do with a stretcher."

A guard entered swiftly with a pliable stretcher that he assembled and deposited on the floor. The haste with which he departed wasn't lost on her.

There was a basin in the corner, but no shower or bath. She took in the gurney laid out with surgical gloves, disinfectant, antiseptic soap, surgical thread, needles, and bandages. "I'll need a local anesthetic."

"We don't have any," Frik said.

Don't have or won't show the prisoner mercy? "I have to stitch him up. You said you were prepared."

"You're going to have to do it without an anesthetic."

"What?" She looked from Frik to Pete. "This is unorthodox."

Pete shrugged. "If you can't work without it, we can always get another nurse."

She spared the man in the chains a look. His face was an unreadable mask.

"Are you sure about being left alone with him?" Pete asked. "My men won't risk it."

"I'm here to help him. I doubt he'll attack me."

Frik snickered. "This is going to be interesting."

A look from Pete shut him up.

"At your own risk, Ilse." Pete pushed Frik ahead of him through the doorway. "Good luck."

The heavy metal door swung shut. She was closed into the space with a man who wasn't a man. Scrap that. He was very much a man, just not human. Not completely. She was frightened, but he needed her help, or he was going to die.

Her heart thumping in her chest, she bent to pick up the key. When she straightened, she caught the prisoner studying her. Gathering all the courage she possessed, she approached him. From close up, he was even more breathtaking. His gaze sparked with something that reminded her of the Highveld electrical storms, of lightning zipping across the sky. Now that she was close enough to touch him, she could see more than blood and grime. Underneath the dirt, bruises marred his ribs. She knew bruises like that. They were caused by fists. The ends of his hair were singed in places. That explained the smell when she'd entered. Her breath caught as realization hit her. He'd been tortured.

"I'm not going to hurt you," she said. "I'm going to tend to your wounds. Will you let me?"

Amusement washed into his stoic expression. "Are you asking for my permission?"

That voice. It was deep and gravelly. He'd spoken with humor, but there was an underlying sensuality to the tone that simultaneously caressed and alarmed her senses. His tone was soft, but it exuded command. It added not only to his allure, but also to the danger emanating from him.

She swallowed. "I'll need to touch you."

"Go ahead." His lips curved into a slow smile. "I won't bite."

She glanced at his wrists. They were secured too high above his head for her to reach. Damn Pete and his agents for not making this easy. She'd have to stand on something. After a quick look around the room, she settled on the portable stretcher. She felt the man's unsettling eyes on her as she pulled the stretcher closer and climbed on top. She had to stretch out to reach his hand. Pressing her body against his was inevitable to maintain her balance.

"Sorry," she mumbled, "but it's difficult to reach. I'll try to hurry."

"By all means, take your time."

With her standing on the stretcher, their eyes were level. As her breasts brushed his chest, the yellow color of his eyes deepened to a golden glow. It was like the rich, dark, liquid gold she'd seen at the mine museum when poured into the form to set. The subtle change had her so mesmerized she forgot what she was doing. Who *was* this beautiful man? What did she know about him other than he wasn't a normal human being? She wasn't a supporter of normalizing or generalizing people. Someone wasn't abnormal simply because he didn't resemble the standards of the majority. Each person was unique. Therefore, the term *normal* seemed redundant, but there was something about this man that shouted danger. Her pulse picked up in response to her thoughts, blood pumping furiously to her frightened heart. She'd be dishonest if she said she wasn't apprehensive.

His gaze shifted to where she could feel the vein in her neck keep pace with her heart. Slowly, he dragged his eyes back to hers. While the golden color had appeared unearthly before, it now looked like something from a fantasy. They seemed to have ignited, sparks popping in their depths like fireflies. Her lips parted on a soundless gasp, more fear bleeding into her veins.

His voice stroked over her senses again. "I'm not going to hurt you."

Could he sense how afraid she was? She might confess it to herself, but she wasn't going to make herself that vulnerable by admitting it to him.

She reached for his wrist, focusing all of her attention on fitting the key into the shackle. "I'm supposed to say that."

A chuckle rumbled in his chest. "You already did."

Ignoring the vibration of that soft, deep laugh she could feel right through her clothes all the way to her bones, she made quick work of unlocking his right wrist. Lowering his arm, he groaned. The return of the circulation would hurt, but at least the position had slowed down the blood loss.

He held open his palm. "Give me the key. It'll be easier for me to finish."

With an inward sigh of relief, she handed over the key and climbed to the floor. He unlocked his left wrist and shook his arms. While he worked on the shackles around his ankles, she pulled the stretcher next to the gurney.

A click sounded followed by the chime of a chain, and then he was free. All that stood between them was a flimsy stretcher. He indeed looked like a man with the strength to tear her limbs apart, but the earnest way in which he'd spoken when he'd said he wouldn't hurt her made her believe him.

She pointed at the stretcher. "Lie down here."

The sensual curve of his lips tilted up. "Is that an order?"

"Yes," she replied sternly. "Do you need help or can you walk alone?"

His answer was to approach her so swiftly she took an involuntary step back. The way he moved was smooth. Unnatural. It reminded her of a panther on the prowl, but in fast forward action.

Holding her gaze, he lowered himself onto the stretcher. "What is your designation?"

"My designation?"

"For you to issue the orders."

She suppressed a smile. "I don't carry any authority here."

"What is your status?"

There was the slightest accent to his English. It was exotic, unlike anything she'd heard.

"I don't understand."

"Your status in society," he repeated. "Are you taken?"

"Taken?"

His eyes roamed the ceiling as he seemed to search for a word. "Married."

"Ah." The smile almost slipped free. "My marital status is private. It's not polite to ask."

"You mean it's impolite to ask a lady if she's attached before you make a…" he squinted, apparently searching for another word, "a move?"

Where *was* he from? His naivety was kind of cute. As for the rest of him, cute wasn't a word she'd use. Hazardously male would be closer to the truth.

"It's inappropriate in our situation," she explained.

"Why?"

She waved between them. "This is professional. Now be quiet. I have to examine you."

Pulling on a pair of surgical gloves, she inspected his shoulder before turning her attention to his side. "No organs seemed to have been damaged, but I would've preferred a scan to be sure."

She shone a light into his eyes. His pupils contracted normally. Some of the veins on the outer extremities had burst. Outrage and compassion filled her anew.

She lowered her voice. "They tortured you, didn't they?"

He didn't reply.

"It's illegal, you know," she said. "You can lay charges."

Wait. That sounded obscure. He was detained in a dungeon, chained, and tortured by the SS, no less. What hope did a prisoner in such circumstances have of exercising his legal rights? None. Whatever dangerous picture the agents had painted, he seemed calm and kind as he lay there, submitting to her probing and prodding which had to hurt like hell.

She straightened with a soft sigh. "Let's get you cleaned up as best as we can."

At the basin, she poured water into a dish and squirted anti-septic soap on the sponge. Being as gentle as she could, she started giving him a sponge bath. As her fingers skimmed over his abdomen, his cock twitched. The reaction was slight, but not so slight that she could miss it. His gaze moved to where his flesh was starting to stiffen before he fixed those eerie golden eyes on her face, again.

She cleared her throat. "Don't worry about it. It's a natural reaction."

"I'm not worried about it. On the contrary."

At her chastising look, his lips parted in a smile. He was perfection, but when he smiled he was pure seduction.

"Do you get that a lot?" he asked.

"It happens in my profession."

"What profession is that?"

"You don't know?"

"No."

"You can't tell from the uniform?"

He eyed her wet tunic. "No."

He definitely wasn't from this planet. "I'm a nurse." With his erection growing between them, she needed to take a distance. She pressed a sterile gauze to his shoulder. Miraculously, it wasn't bleeding as much as a wound of that depth should've.

"Turn around," she said in her best professional voice. "If you can't lie down on your stomach, you can sit. Here, let me help you."

Lying on his stomach, he looked like one of Michelangelo's marble statues. Maybe David with his perfectly defined back muscles, broad shoulders, and narrow waist. It was best not to go into a detailed description of his ass.

She changed the water several times, until he was as clean as he was going to get with a sponge bath.

"You can turn back now," she said when she was done.

She gathered the disinfectant and sterile gauzes. "Ready?"

He grinned. "Seeing that you're my *best shot*, yes."

Eyeing the gaping wound on his shoulder, she caught her lip

between her teeth. It was going to hurt like a bitch. A hiss escaped his lips when she poured disinfectant over the wound.

"I'm sorry," she said.

"Why? You didn't cause the wounds."

"I'm sorry that it hurts. I'm sorry I can't give you something for the pain."

Something shifted in his eyes. "The guard who attacked me, how is he doing?"

"I don't know." She glanced at the mirror. "They didn't tell me anything."

"You didn't lie when you said you don't have authority here. You're not part of this organization."

"I work at a hospital. They only brought me in to take care of your injuries."

Donning a new pair of gloves, she threaded the needle with the surgical thread. Staples would've been easier, but the cut was deep. Good, old-fashioned thread would be more effective. She hated that she had to hurt him more.

"It won't be worse than what I've already suffered," he said as if he could read her thoughts.

Taking a deep breath, she inserted the needle into his skin at the top of the cut, pulling the thread through as carefully as she could. Aside from the occasional grunt, he said nothing as she first stitched up his shoulder and then the long cut on his shin. He didn't need stitches in his side. A skin adhesive was sufficient.

When she'd applied an antibacterial ointment and bandages to the cuts, she stepped back to examine her work. He needed antibiotics and a tetanus shot. He needed to be in a hospital bed under observation. It went against every grain of her humanity to leave him like this.

She couldn't help herself from reaching out with a soothing touch, laying her hand on his forehead. "How are you doing?"

He sat up slowly, turning sideways on the stretcher so she was standing between his legs.

Giving her a beseeching look, he said, "You've been very kind, but if I don't get back to my pod, I'll be dead in a few days."

"Your pod?" This situation was getting more bizarre by the second. Her voice came out as a whisper. "What *happened* to you?"

"My plane crashed." He uttered *plane* carefully, as if it was a new word to him.

"What?" she shrieked. "You survived a plane crash?"

A voice boomed through the space, making her jump. "Secure the prisoner."

There had to be a microphone hidden in the room. She had no doubt the agents were listening in on their conversation.

The prisoner wrapped his big hand around her wrist, gently holding her in place. "Tell me your name."

The touch came as a surprise. Already on edge, it made her jump.

"Tell me," he urged.

She wet her dry lips. "Ilse."

"Ilse." He said her name slowly and meticulously, as if he was not only testing the sound on his tongue, but also committing it to memory.

Questions flooded her mind. "Who *are* you?"

"Secure the prisoner. Now."

He growled at the mirror, his expression so fierce it sent ripples of shivers over her skin, but when he looked back at her, his gaze turned soft again. Intense. Like his touch. Under the circle of his fingers her skin burned.

"Who are you?" she asked again, more urgently.

Before he could utter another word, the door flew open, and several guards armed with automatic rifles stormed inside. In a flash, much faster than humanly possible, the prisoner was on his feet. He yanked her behind him, placing his body in front of hers and snarling like a wild animal at the men.

Pete entered the room, pushing the men aside. "Inject him."

"Wait!" Ilse stepped around the prisoner, his fingers still like a steel vice on her wrist. "He needs to lie down. Maybe you don't understand the severity of his injuries, but--"

"The prisoner *will* be secured," Pete interjected, "or we will sedate him to do so."

She gasped. "Sedate him? I thought you said you didn't have anesthetic."

"It's not the same," Pete said. "This substance won't be kind on his nervous system." He gave the prisoner a pointed look. "It's time for Nurse Gouws to leave. Let her go."

Frik cracked the knuckles of his good hand. "Give me the needle. This time, asshole," he said to the prisoner, "try not to choke in your vomit when you wake."

"I'll secure him," Ilse said quickly, "if he'll let me." She looked at her patient with a pleading look.

The loathing disappeared from his face as he turned it from Frik to her.

"Please," she begged. "I don't want them to hurt you. It won't help your healing."

In wordless agreement, he loosened his fingers from her wrist.

"Get up against that wall," Frik shouted.

"Take it easy," Ilse chided. "He understood you."

The prisoner backed up to the wall, his eerie eyes on Frik. What she saw in those depths made her tremble. The man spread his legs and lifted his arms in silent surrender. It crushed her heart to see him like that. Whatever his crimes, she didn't believe he was the monster Pete and Frik had claimed. Underneath the stoic veneer, there was humor and kindness. Her gut trusted him. Not Frik. Definitely not after the injuries she'd witnessed. The cuts could be contributed to a crash, but not the bruises on his ribs and over his kidneys.

"Do it, nurse," Frik said.

She advanced slowly, drawing out the inevitable with seconds. Staring into his eyes, she mouthed, "I'm sorry," before closing the shackle around one ankle and then the other. Seeing that his wrists were too high for her to reach, Pete finished the job.

"Take her back to the parking," Pete said to Frik. Then to her, "Agent Pillay will take you home."

"I'll have to come back to dress the wounds," she said.

"That won't be--" Frik started, but Pete cut him short.

"We'll see. If needed, we know where to find you." With a curt nod, he dismissed her.

She was about to walk through the door when the prisoner's voice stopped her.

"Drako."

"What?" She turned back to him.

"My name is Drako."

Beside her, Frik uttered an ugly laugh. "Well, I'll be damned. Looks like what we needed all along wasn't torture, but a pretty nurse."

Pete slapped the back of his head. "Get out of my sight before I fire your ass."

"What?" Frik huffed.

"He made a joke," Pete said to Ilse, "albeit not a very good one."

It was better not to reply. With a last look at the prisoner, who now had a name, she left the building with Frik.

Drako.

She repeated the name in her mind. What kind of a name was that? What was going on here? What were the agents hiding? Would she ever see Drako again?

4

The heavy chains on Drako's legs drew tight as he shuffled down the corridor. They were short, allowing him only small, uncomfortable steps. Attached to each shackle was another short chain with a heavy weight he dragged behind him. Frik shoved the barrel of his rifle between his shoulder blades, making him stumble. He flung his head around with a snarl, which only incited a laugh from the agent. Since waking up in chains, Frik had beaten him and given him countless electric shocks. Revenge for the guard's broken wrist, he assumed. There was also a spark of perverse excitement in the Earthling's eyes whenever he doled out the torture. No doubt, he took pleasure from it. A defective psychological trait. He could easily strangle the pitiful man with the chains that bound his wrists, but they were taking him to his pod--at last--and he needed to know where it was too badly to evoke the humans' anger right now.

His mission had been to conduct reconnaissance on Earth. His planet, Krina, was dying, and the Krinar needed a new, habitable home. Life on Earth had been instigated by his compatriots, and although he was too young to have taken part in the experiment, he'd learned all about it before setting off on his mission. His feedback was not concerning the nature of food sources or other physical means of survival––he was not a biologist, and there were other Krinar for that––but to report on human behavior. He was to gather first-hand knowledge of their comportment so that the Elders could access how easy, or difficult, integration would be. Another shove from Frik and he was starting to think humans didn't deserve the planet they inhabited. If the SS were to be ambassadors of their kind, he'd put a recommendation forward that the species be extinguished, as cohabitation with such a cruel and underdeveloped race seemed highly improbable, if not dysfunctional. So far, they'd given him no reason to plead for their lives—except for one.

The female they'd brought to tend to his wounds. Ilse. He rolled the name around in his mind, as he did in all the hours they kept him chained in their prison. It kept him sane. She was different. She was kind and gentle. Soft. In body and soul. He'd smelled her distress at causing him pain. It had a fragrance of burnt sugar. He could smell her fear, too, but she was brave, brave enough to defend him against her own kind. There were other smells far more intoxicating than her care and bravery. Her womanly essence had drifted to him the minute she'd entered his cell, sweet and seductive, unlike anything he'd experienced. The perfume of her skin was like the petals of a rose, a bloom unique to Earth. Beneath that, there was the promise of her blood that drew him like a deranged vampire. He'd drunk the occasional synthetic blood at the Krina bars and enjoyed it as much as any other Krinar, but he'd been told nothing compared to the real thing. It would seem the hearsay wasn't unfounded, because he'd never been more tempted to taste anything in his life. He'd filled the long hours with no distinction between day or night with images of the impossibly small, curvy woman, imagining what it would be like to touch her everywhere, to kiss the fragrant skin of her neck, to run his tongue over her most sensitive parts, and to sink his teeth into the delicate vein in her neck. Just a taste. He'd meant it when he'd said he didn't want to hurt her. If the rumors were anything to go by, biting her would bring her pleasure if they were coupling during the act. The thought alone had him go hard. It took extreme concentration to force down his dick. The guards who escorted him to the station where they kept his pod weren't the audience he wanted for his hardening dick. It was an exotic creature with cloudy blue eyes, golden hair, generous hips, perfectly rounded breasts, and the softest hands he'd ever felt. She was nothing like the tall, lean, and toned Krinar females he'd coupled with. He couldn't help but wonder what it would feel like to settle between her legs and take her deep with everything he had––fingers, tongue, teeth, and cock.

"We're here," Pete said, holding up a hand to halt the entourage.

He punched in a code on a wall panel, and a metal door slid open to reveal a large warehouse with broken windows.

Drako would have no problem finding the place again. He'd carefully noted the path and stored it in his brain. They were on the upper level of the building in which they kept him on what appeared to be a closed rooftop. From the dirty and broken windowpanes, he could see a helicopter outside on a concrete slab. After assessing possible dangers and escape routes, his priority was locating his pod. He didn't have to wait long. At Pete's command, the guards drew a curtain aside. His pod stood in the middle of the floor. The left side was gone, due to the explosion. Irreparable. What concerned him more were the men in white coats surrounding his craft. They carried all kinds of ancient-looking tools. The dashboard that contained the communication system had been dismantled, the pieces lying neatly next to one another on a sheet on the floor.

He jerked forward with rage, only to receive the heel of Frik's boot on his kidney.

"My technicians spent forty-eight hours on your plane," Pete said, "without any luck. None of it makes sense. Show them how to repair it, and you can use it to fly home, wherever that is."

He could smell the lie. It had a foul odor, like rotten food. His lip curled up in disgust.

"Well, buddy?" Pete said, giving him a slap on the shoulder. "What do you say?"

Falseness added another dimension of rot to the smell that poured from the man's pores.

Drako gave him a level look. "I can't assist in your request."

Pete's brow scrunched. "What?"

"I'm not a technician," Drako said. "I don't have the knowledge to fix the … plane." Which was the truth.

"He's lying," Frik yelled. "I'll get the truth out of him."

"Like you did when Agent Morrison lost his arm?" Pete said. "No," he shook his head, "I have a feeling he's telling the truth."

"Then he's worth nothing to us."

Pete turned to Drako. "Can you contact your planet?"

"No." Not at the moment. If he managed to fix the distress signal feature on the communication device, maybe.

Pete grabbed his uninjured shoulder. "Tell us where you're from."

What damage could it do? They'd find out sooner than later. Anyway, he would eventually escape, and when he did, he wasn't going to leave any evidence of the Krinar's existence behind. It would be a few guards and agents' wild story with nothing to show for it.

"Krina," he replied.

Frik looked at Pete. "I've never heard of such a planet."

"You wouldn't have," Drako said. "It's in a different galaxy."

Frik gave a snort-laugh. "You expect us to believe that?"

"Yes." The man's shortsighted vision was another one of his defects. Drako couldn't truly blame him, seeing that the Krinar had kept their existence a secret for so long humans believed they were the only intelligent species in the universe. "I am a Krinar."

"A Krinar, eh?" Frik chuckled. "He can't repair his craft, and he can't contact his *people*. I say we give him to research, see what they find if they cut him open."

"I'd like to have a word with Frik in private," Pete said.

At the command, the other guards scattered to the far end of the hall, out of earshot, but their bullets still in range.

Pete took Frik's arm and pulled him aside. It was out of human earshot, but with Drako's enhanced hearing, he had no problem following the conversation.

"He's inhumanly strong," Pete said in a hushed tone.

"All the more reason to let the science guys slice him up. The sooner the better."

"You don't understand. We can't use his technology, and we can't contact his home to trade him for their advanced weapons or knowledge, but we're sitting on a goldmine."

"Even if the metal of his plane is stronger than any reinforced titanium, what use is it if we can't source or replicate it?"

Pete glanced at Drako. "It's not the metal I'm interested in selling. It's the man."

Frik scratched his head. "The man?"

"We have the strongest soldier the world has ever seen in our possession."

Frik's gaze lit up. "You mean sell *him*?"

"Why would we sell one man if we can sell an army?"

"I'm not following. You've lost me."

Pete brought his head closer to Frik's. "DNA. We can make our own army. Countries would pay a fortune for it. Imagine the power we'll have. I'm talking world manipulation."

"Fucking brilliant," Frik exclaimed. "We can sell the DNA for cloning."

"Exactly."

"I like you more and more, boss."

"I'd have to run it past the president, but in my experience, he's not a man to shy away from money or power, no matter how unorthodox it is."

"Just make sure you get us each a big cut, enough to retire before word gets out and other countries let their spies loose on us."

"Don't worry. We'll both have enough money to disappear forever. As far as I'm concerned, this operation never existed."

Frik nodded his approval. "Good thinking."

"Take him back to the cell," Pete called to the guards. He addressed Frik in a softer voice. "Take a blood sample. We should be able to extract the DNA from that."

Drako's Krinar blood seethed. Of all the foul, under-handed manners in the universe, these humans displayed the worse. Not only were they cruel, but also greedy. He suppressed a wry chuckle. They were in for a surprise if they thought they'd clone him.

5

No matter how much Ilse immersed herself in work, she couldn't get her mind off the man in the SS dungeon. She'd gone home with icy shivers running down her spine a warm shower hadn't alleviated. Every time she closed her eyes, she saw Drako spread-eagled against the wall, his haunting yellow eyes drilling into hers. "If I don't get back to my pod, I'm as good as dead," he'd said.

Was she losing her mind? It would've helped if she could talk to Caitlin who she considered a good friend, but there was no mistaking Pete's warning. Talking could get her killed, run over, or something else that would look like an accident, not to mention putting Caitlin at risk. Already, she'd been looking over her shoulder all the way to work.

When her shift ended at four, she'd worked herself to near collapsing, but still her mind lingered on Drako. How was he coping? What were they doing to him? Where had they found him? She both prayed Agent Pillay would come back for her and that he wouldn't. She simultaneously dreaded returning to that dungeon and not going back. In the slim chance they'd fetch her to check on Drako, she put in an order for painkillers and antibiotics at the medicine depot.

She was changing out of her uniform when Caitlin rapped on the change room door.

"Hey," Ilse said in greeting.

"What's this?" Caitlin held up the order. "Depot asked me to sign it off."

"It's for the prisoner, you know, the one the agent took me to see yesterday."

"Mm-mm." Caitlin leaned her hip against the doorframe. "I wanted to ask about that, but today I didn't have five minutes to pee. How did it go?"

Ilse brushed her hair and redid the braid. "Fine."

"You haven't been yourself all day. You're as jumpy as a Mexican bean."

She forced a smile. "Just tired."

"Told you to get more sleep."

"That's exactly what I'm planning on doing after running some errands."

Caitlin signed the form on her clipboard and handed it to Ilse. "Here you go."

"I'll swing by the depot, and then I'm off. Call me if you need an extra hand on the midnight shift." She picked up her bag.

"Uh-uh." Caitlin pointed a finger at her. "Sleep."

"Yes, boss."

"That's better. I don't want to worry my ass off about you."

Ilse waved over her shoulder. "You worry too much."

While she waited for the order at the medicine depot, she eyed the staff on duty until she spotted the new pharmacist graduate.

"Annemarie, right?"

The girl approached the counter. "Have we met?"

"I'm Ilse. Welcome to the team. How are you enjoying the job so far?"

"It's all right, I guess."

Ilse glanced around to check that no one was within earshot. "I meant to ask you something."

The girl looked uncomfortable. "I don't fabricate drugs for recreational purposes."

"No, nothing like that. I've heard that you know about a black market for medicine."

Annemarie's cheeks blanched. "Who said that?"

"Rumors. You know how the staff talks in the canteen."

"Sorry to disappoint you, but I don't know what you're talking about."

"Look, we're out of Rifampin. Our new batch was stolen, and there's this old lady who missed out on her monthly dose. I promised I'd get her some."

Her voice rose in panic. "You're planning on buying it from the black market?"

"Check the inventory. A new batch isn't due until next month."

"You're serious?"

"I promised. She came all the way from Alexandra only to be sent away empty-handed."

The girl bit her lip. "Look, I've only heard some rumors."

"I'll take my chances."

"You didn't hear it from me."

"My lips are sealed."

Annemarie leaned over the counter, lowering her voice to a whisper. "There's a shop called Amina's Fabrics at the Oriental Plaza. Ask for red silk from India."

"Thanks."

Annemarie opened her mouth, but before she could say something, the pharmacist on duty returned with Ilse's order.

Annemarie gave Ilse a resigned look. "Be careful."

"It was good to meet you."

She signed for the medicine and made her way to the parking lot. The Plaza closed at five. If she didn't get stuck in traffic, she could make it there in under an hour. Knowing the back roads through Brixton, it took her less then thirty-five minutes to pull up at the Plaza. The traffic was already heavy with the office workers who started at seven and knocked off at four. Peak-hour would erupt at five. She didn't look forward to getting stuck in the traffic in town, but there was no helping it.

Making her way through the arched entrance of the open-air market, she stopped to get her bearings. She hadn't been here since shopping with her mother as a child. The area had gone backward in the last few years, becoming too risky for carefree shopping. The place was exactly as she remembered. The food stalls were near the entrance. The fragrance of fried samosas and curry hung in the air.

"Cheap watches," a vendor called from a jewelry stand. "A Rolex for the pretty lady."

She made her way through the stalls of homeware, clothes, and spices toward the closed area where the textiles were sold.

"Ten percent discount. Today only!"

"Pretty dresses. Touch them. See? Real chiffon."

"Tandoori spices. Ready mixed. No wedding ring, I see. The way to a man's heart is through his stomach. Here, take a sample."

At last, the escalators came into sight. She hurried to the first floor that ran in a square around the ground level market. Anima's Fabrics was located in one of the farthest corners, next to a pet shop.

"Hello," a parrot cried from his cage in front of the pet shop when she entered Amina's store.

A bell chimed over the door. The fragrance of incense and fabric greeted her. A fan stirred hot air around the room. A friendly-looking woman wearing a sari approached her with a smile. Her gray hair was twisted into a bun at the nape of her neck.

"Good day. What can I do for you? We have beautiful wedding dress silk on sale. Or maybe some blue for an evening gown?" The woman took a roll of fabric from a shelf and held it in front of Ilse.

"Look at that, how it brings out your eyes. Yes, look. Come." She turned her toward a mirror fitted on the wall.

"Actually," Ilse cleared her throat, "I'm looking for some red silk from India."

The women's hands stilled a moment before she returned the fabric to the shelf. Her eyes turned hard as she called to the back. "Ismael, here's a customer for you."

A young man with a pimply face exited from behind a curtain. He held the curtain aside. "Through here." With a smile, he waved her into a small, windowless room.

The woman mumbled an insult under her breath and turned her back on them.

"Sorry about that," he said once she was inside. "My mother doesn't like that I run my business from the back."

You bet.

He pushed a pair of gold-framed spectacles onto his nose and sat down behind a desk the size of an apple box. "What do you need?"

"Rifampin."

"Ah. You're in luck. I got in a new batch. How much do you need?"

"How much does it cost?"

"For you, a special price. One thousand five hundred rand for thirty capsules."

She nearly choked. "What? That's three times the retail price."

"Yeah, but the demand warrants the price. I guarantee you won't find it elsewhere. I'm the sole stocker. Go try the hospitals and see for yourself."

"Don't I know," she gritted out.

It took all her self-control not to call him a thief who robbed poor, sick people of their health. If she thought it would make a difference, she'd report him, but the police were often involved, taking kickbacks from the black market dealers.

Grudgingly, she dug the money from her purse. "I only have enough for one box."

"No worries." He flashed her a gold-toothed smile. "You can always come back when you have more cash. I give a ten percent discount to my loyal customers."

After stashing the money in his back pocket, he took a key from the other pocket and unlocked a cabinet. He removed the Rifampin and sealed it in a brown bag.

Pushing it over the desk, he said, "It'll be five rand for the bag."

She stared at him incredulously. About to say something insulting, she swallowed it back. The faster she could get out of here, the better. She took the coin from her purse and left it on the desk. She left without a greeting.

"Thanks for your business," he called after her in a cheerful voice.

The woman looked up from behind the counter. "Junkie," she mumbled as Ilse exited the shop.

Only outside did she breathe easier. She kept on looking over her shoulder, not knowing if she expected to see an SS agent or police officer. If a police officer arrested her for illegal black market dealings, she'd have to buy her way out, and although she wasn't suffering financially, she didn't have a lot of money in her savings account. She only relaxed once she was safely locked in her car. It was too late to drive to Alexandra. It would have to wait until tomorrow.

As expected, she hit the peak-hour traffic, getting stuck in a bottleneck outside the Plaza. Instead of heading back to Brixton, she decided to go via Newtown. With the city center mostly being a ghost town, the traffic should be lighter. She turned the radio to a classical station to soothe her nerves. Every part of her body was clenched tight. She couldn't shake the feeling of pending doom. Her tension only got worse as she looked up and spotted the Nelson Mandela Bridge that connected Braamfontein with downtown. She stared at it for a long time, the time it took for the traffic light to change three times, to be exact. Agent Pillay had driven for no more than ten to fifteen minutes after he'd made her put on the blindfold on that bridge, which meant the building where the SS kept Drako couldn't be far. Several shivers ran in succession down her spine. Her gaze darted around the skyscrapers, many of which were deserted. When crime had moved in, businesses had moved out. She followed the road from the bridge with her eyes to where it circled before the mine dumps and continued east, and then she spotted it--a black SS helicopter parked on a rooftop. For a moment, she forgot to breathe. The building was the old, abandoned police headquarters where political prisoners had allegedly been tortured. It was supposed to be deserted, only it wasn't.

6

The door rattled and opened. Drako lifted his head. He'd rested as much as he could in the upright position. He didn't need as much sleep as humans, but he couldn't sustain his strength for long without water. Eventually, he'd also need nutrients. He didn't need an evaluation from a medical expert to know his wounds were infected. He could feel the foreign bacteria invading his cells.

Expecting Frik to enter with more of his questions and torture, he blinked in surprise as a female carrying a tray covered with a cloth walked into the room. The door slammed shut behind her. She was very appealing, even by Krinar standards. Her smooth skin was the color of mocha. Black hair curled down her back, and her dark eyes were framed with long lashes. Judging by the size and unnatural firmness of her breasts, they were cosmetically enhanced. She wore a short dress and heels so high they had to come with a safety warning. Toned legs flexed as she swayed her hips. Her lips were glossy, painted with a shiny veneer. Despite her physical beauty, her odor was offensive. Her blood was pumped full of chemicals. He could smell it, even from the distance.

"Hey, honey."

She spoke with a sultry voice, but he could smell her fear.

She took a step closer, holding out the tray. "You hungry?"

Her voice was deep and raspy. A drug humans called nicotine carried on her breath. When he didn't reply, she carried the tray to the gurney and swiped some of the medical supplies aside to deposit it. She lifted the cloth and picked up a bowl and spoon. A sickening fragrance of dead flesh filled the space. She closed the distance and lifted the bowl for him to smell.

"Soup," she said. "It's beef."

He didn't bother to explain that Krinar didn't consume flesh. He doubted Pete was going to cater to his fussiness.

The woman ran her gaze over his form, her eyes lingering on his crotch. They widened slightly before glancing fleetingly at the mirror. "It's not poisoned. I promise. Look." She dipped the spoon into the broth and brought it to her lips. She opened wide and swallowed. "See? It's safe. You should eat."

When there was no reaction from him, she huffed and left the bowl on the floor.

Propping her hands on her hips, she looked back at the tray. "Orange juice, then?"

He swallowed. His throat was so dry he could drink his own piss.

"Good," she said with an approving nod, obviously taking the small gesture as a yes.

She walked back to the gurney and returned with a paper cup in which a thin tube resembling a straw was inserted. It was long enough to reach his lips. The smell confirmed she hadn't lied. Oranges were exotic to Krina, but he'd studied the Earth food types and their synthetically created flavors and perfumes before his mission.

He drank greedily until the cup was empty.

"Right, big boy," she purred, setting the cup down next to the bowl. "Hungry for something else?"

The way she jutted her breasts at him suggested she was offering something other than food. He growled from deep within his chest when she neared, not wishing her hands on him.

She chuckled. "No need to get all animalistic, now. It'll be fun. I promise."

She was making too many promises for her own good. The smell of her perfume was too strong, but not strong enough to mask the chemicals that soured her blood. It repulsed him. He grimaced when she went down on her haunches and reached for his cock. She curled her fingers around him, stroking up and down.

"Remove your hands from my body," he said, his voice tight with anger.

"Now, now," she cooed, not stopping her movements, "just relax."

When his cock remained flaccid, she directed it to her lips and opened her mouth. He gritted his teeth against the unsavory sensation as the wet heat of her mouth surrounded him. It wasn't that he didn't like oral stimulation. Like every other man, he loved it, just not with her. The food might not be poisoned, but her tongue was. He didn't care for it. Everything about her seemed artificial.

She spat him out with a pop, letting him see her slimy saliva on his skin. "That's it, baby." She stuffed him back down her throat, panting and making mewling noises. Pop. His limp dick fell from her lips. "You make me so hot."

He winced when she lapped at him, dragging her tongue over the sensitive head. The falseness of her words added to the bitterness of her infected blood. Her lies smelled foul. No female arousal permeated the room, only frustration as she sucked harder and took him deeper while throwing a concerned glance at the mirror. She abandoned his cock and attacked his balls, sucking and licking with vigor.

"Come, baby. Get hard for me."

When that didn't work, she popped out her breasts, but the sight of those curves only repulsed him further. Wasn't his style.

"You want me naked, honey?" she said, dragging her nails over his ass.

No reaction came from his cock. Not even a twitch.

"Argh!" She slapped his dick and pushed to her feet. "What the hell are you? Impotent? You prefer men?"

"It's nothing personal," he said, "but you're not––How do you say?––my *type*."

"Fuck you." She flipped her dress over her breasts and stomped to the door. "Let me out. I'm done in here."

The door opened to reveal a red-faced, stiff-dicked Frik. Apparently, she was his type.

"I thought you said you were good, whore," he snapped.

"I am." Her gaze dropped to the front of Frik's pants. "There's your proof."

"Shut up, slut."

She held out her palm. "I want my money."

"You're not getting paid. You didn't do the job."

She stretched herself out in an indignant pose. "He," she pointed a long, varnished nail at Drako, "is seriously fucked. Good luck for getting any reaction out of him."

He grabbed her arm and jerked her over the doorstep. "Get out."

Before he could close the door, Drako said, "By the way, I'm vegan. You forgot to ask about my dietary requirements."

"Shut your mousetrap, freak."

Frik banged the door so hard the metal creaked.

Drako grinned. He couldn't help himself from getting a rise out of the man. He'd probably pay for it later, but it was worth the whole two seconds it had lasted.

A moment later, the door opened and a furious Frik stalked inside. He kicked the soup bowl, sending it flying through the air.

The porcelain crashed against the wall, the broth spilling down the concrete and onto the floor.

He grabbed the electric prod that was hooked onto his belt. "Let's see how hard you get when I stick this up your ass and send a few volts to your balls."

"Frik." Pete rushed inside and grabbed his wrist. "Calm down. All this shocking can't be helping him to get it up."

"The DNA might as well be Morse code, and the whore we hired didn't work. What's your plan, now, huh?"

Pete dragged him to the door and shut it. Their argument continued in the hallway, the thick walls and metal not masking their words from Drako's hearing.

"We can't fucking decipher the DNA," Frik yelled, "or whatever is running through that alien's veins, because it sure as hell doesn't look like any DNA I've ever seen, and now we don't have semen, either."

"We'll get the semen and sell it for artificial insemination," Pete said in a placating tone.

Drako chuckled quietly to himself. They were in for an even bigger surprise. He wasn't going to tell them his sperm was incompatible with humans and they were going to look like the biggest clowns in history if they attempted to sell it. Besides, the longer they remained ignorant, the longer he'd live. The minute they realized he was of no use to them in any way, he was dead.

"If it doesn't work, we're going to have to kill him," Frik said, confirming Drako's conclusion. "You know that, don't you? After what we did to him, there's no way we can let him go."

Pete sighed. "Yeah. I know. Don't worry. It'll work. Before you know it, we'll be selling superhuman sperm to every government in the world, but only after we've harvested enough to fill our own sperm bank and reinforce our army. Just lay off the violence for a while. With the way you're carrying on, we won't have a sperm donor for long."

Frik laughed softly. "I look forward to milking that

motherfucking extraterrestrial's dick until it shrivels up and drops off." ·

Drako ground his teeth. Incompatible with a human ovum or not, he'd rather die before he gave them a drop of his sperm.

"I think I have another plan," Pete said slowly.

Damnation. He had to escape. Fast.

IT WAS after seven when Ilse pulled up at her house in Milpark, not far from the hospital. It was small, but it was hers, bought and paid off with the money her parents' had left her. More than that, it was home, a place where she felt happy, safe, and relaxed. She exhaled in relief and rubbed her aching neck. For the whole two hours she'd been stuck in traffic, she'd thought about one thing only—the SS building and the man held inside. She wanted to help Drako, but how? How could she fight the SS? Who would believe her claim that the Secret Service was holding a man of a different species in a deserted building? If she spilled the beans, how long would she live?

She was so preoccupied with thoughts of Drako and what to do, she didn't notice the man sitting on her porch until she'd exited her car. Her heart jerked when she recognized Agent Pete Evans. It was too late to get back into the car and speed away, because their eyes had already locked. She couldn't pretend she hadn't seen him.

As if sensing her hesitation, he got to his feet with a smile. "Good evening, Ilse."

She pushed through the garden gate, hoping her face didn't give away her fear. "Hello, Pete."

He regarded her with his hands shoved into his pockets as she walked down the path and climbed the steps. "You're not asking what I'm doing here."

"That's because you can only be here for one reason. You want me to check on your prisoner."

He gave her a crooked smile. "In fact, there is something else."

He indicated the wicker chair facing his, as if it was his home and his right to extend hospitality. When she'd taken a seat, he sat down and crossed his legs. On edge, she kept alert, thankful they were outside in the open and he hadn't asked her to let him inside.

"You're a clever woman, Ilse. You must know Drako isn't your average human."

Damn. Feigning ignorance was over. He knew she knew the truth, and that could get her killed.

"Don't worry," he said. "Nothing will happen to you as long as you keep your mouth shut."

She took a deep breath, forcing her voice to sound normal and not as scared as she felt. "Is this why you're here? To warn me?"

"I'm here to ask your help."

"With what?"

"An experiment."

Her throat tightened. "What kind of experiment?"

He leaned forward and steeped his fingers together. "This may sound bizarre, but Drako claims he's from another planet, and I believe him. He landed in the Ellis Park Stadium in a flying craft no one on Earth has ever seen."

Drako had told the truth when he'd said he'd survived a crash. "Are you saying he's an ... an extraterrestrial?"

"We believe so. We also believe he and his kind mean us harm. He's a very dangerous man, Ilse. He killed one of our agents with his bare hands, literally ripping him apart."

She shuddered at the image.

"We need to keep him detained for mankind's safety," he continued. "Imagine what a whole planet of his kind could do to us if they all descend on Earth."

"What are you saying?" she asked with rising panic.

"We need to be prepared. Invasion has always been on the charts, but now it's a real possibility."

"Prepared how?"

"We need to match them in strength."

"I'm not getting where you're going with this."

"His DNA is too foreign for us to work with. We need his sperm."

She reeled in shock. "You want to use his genetics to enhance the human race?"

"More or less."

"This is your experiment?"

"Yes."

She didn't like where this was going. "What do you need from me?"

"I need you to take a sperm sample."

To tell him she wasn't compliant was signing her death warrant. "That's not part of my usual professional duties."

He gave her a penetrating stare. "I'm not talking *professional duties*, here. We've already tried all the mechanical equipment for sperm extraction, including e-stim. We've even hired a prostitute. Nothing works."

She flinched at the prostitute part.

"We couldn't help but notice that our prisoner seems to be partial to you."

Her body turned cold in the heat of the summer evening. "It was just a biological reaction to touch."

"No one or nothing else has managed to evoke a similar *biological* reaction. That's why we're counting on you."

"Are you asking me to do it … naturally?" she asked in disbelief.

"Yes."

"Without his consent?"

"He's not human, Nurse Gouws," he said harshly. "Don't think of him as a man. Think of him as an animal, a predator set on wiping out our race. Our laws don't apply to him."

"It doesn't change the principle," she exclaimed softly.

"All is fair in love and war, and this is definitely war."

"It remains immoral."

"Let me put it this way. If we can't use him for this experiment, he's a liability to our country—to our world."

Ice filled every pore of her body. If Drako couldn't deliver sperm, they were going to kill him. Now that she knew, she was a liability, too. If she disagreed, Pete would have no choice but to kill her. Dear God. It was like being trapped in a terrifying thriller. She wiped her clammy palms on her thighs. Even if she objected to this horrendous experiment with every fiber of her being, she had to play for time. For Drako, but also for herself. She had to make her compliance look real. Pete was no fool.

Feigning a calm she didn't feel, she asked, "What's in it for me?"

The half-smile returned to his face. "Name your price."

She grabbed the first ridiculously big number that came up in her mind. "One million."

Without batting an eye, he said, "Deal," extending a hand.

Shaking his hand made her feel sick. She had to inhale several times not to empty her stomach. Her skin crawled where he'd touched her.

"I'll throw in a bonus," he said, "and organize an offshore bank account so the money can't be traced."

She forced herself to sound grateful. "That's kind of you."

"I knew it would be a pleasure doing business with you. You're a logical and reasonable young woman." He got up. "Shall we go?"

"Now?"

"Is there any time better than the present?"

She needed time to think, to devise a plan, but to refuse would look suspicious. She had no choice but to follow suit and push to her feet. "I suppose you're right. I'm just apprehensive."

"Understandable." His look was sympathetic. "I know the task isn't agreeable. Just think that it's for your country while you're doing it."

"Exactly how are you expecting me to collect his sperm?"

His stare was direct. "In any way necessary."

"I hope it will work," she said through dry lips.

"For his sake, I hope so, too." He took a blindfold from his pocket and held it to her. "You know what to do."

7

The smell of roses, female sensuality, and apprehension reached Drako even before the door opened. He knew who'd be walking through it, but he wasn't prepared for the sight as Ilse stepped into the room. Unlike yesterday, she wore a tight pair of pants that hugged her hips and an off-shoulder sweater that exposed one, creamy shoulder. That small part of flesh bared to him was a thousand times more sensual than the tits that had been flashed in his face.

"Ilse." He ran his gaze from the top of her head all the way to her feet, taking in every inch that was hidden beneath the layers of clothes.

"Drako."

The sound of his name on her lips did things to him that weren't supposed to happen while he was chained to a wall. He wanted to feel the warmth that flooded his groin while his hands ran over her body, exploring the womanly need his touch would evoke.

"You're back," he said.

She toyed with the end of the braid that hung over her shoulder. "I brought you medicine."

Wicked images of coiling that braid around his fist while pounding into her from behind made blood rush to his cock. Only sheer willpower prevented it from rising instantly. She was here to treat him professionally, and he didn't want to scare her away with his inappropriate lust. He craved the feel of her soft hands on his body too much. Instead of moving forward and fulfilling his impatient wish, she simply stood there, looking uncertain. Maybe she wasn't as brave as she'd seemed yesterday.

Desire made his voice thick. "You better come closer."

Her lashes lifted, revealing those lovely eyes the color of her planet's sky. "Excuse me?"

Breathtaking. "If you're going to give me medicine, you better come closer."

"Oh." She sounded out of breath. "I was going to do that."

He frowned at her nervousness. "Told you already, I won't bite."

She scratched around in an oversized bag slung over her shoulder and took out two bottles. "Painkillers and antibiotics." She flashed a defiant look at the mirror as she said it.

"Are you going to uncuff me?"

He sure as hell hoped so. It would give him another opportunity to touch her, as warped as it may be to use the situation for his personal, physical interests.

"Yes," she replied with another look at the mirror.

Immediately, the door opened and a guard threw the key on the floor before shutting it again. She dropped her bag to pick up the key, her pants stretching over her ass. The sight quickened his pulse. The smell of her blood made him wild. Fresh and clean, it was stronger than any aphrodisiac. It didn't help that he was half-starved and dehydrated.

Like the day before, she climbed on top of the stretcher to reach the cuff around his right wrist. He did the rest. She ordered him to the stretcher and made him sit down.

"I'm going to clean your wounds," she said, always explaining her actions before touching him.

He couldn't get enough of watching her. While she worked, he drank in her features. Tiny like a doll, she looked breakable. He'd have to be extra careful with her if he ever got the chance of taking it beyond professional. The improbability of the notion made his chest pinch with an uncomfortable ache. He'd escape, leave this planet, and never see her again.

"Shit," she mumbled as she unwrapped the bandage on his shoulder.

He tore his gaze away from her eyes to inspect the damage that had her biting her lip so hard. As he'd suspected, the wound was infected.

She inhaled deeply. Shaking two pills from each of the bottles, she handed them to him. "Take this. I'll get you some water."

She filled a plastic cup at the basin and held it to his lips. He was so thirsty he drank all of it without taking the pills. Understanding mixed with pain in her eyes. She filled the cup twice more for him, ensuring that he'd swallowed the pills.

Gently, she pressed around the wound. "It doesn't look good."

"It's infected," he said.

She replied softly without meeting his eyes. "Yes."

"You did your best."

"You need..." She swallowed and looked away. Lowering her voice to a whisper, she continued, "You need an operation. If you survived a crash, there could be splintered bone or shrapnel lodged in the muscle tissue."

His back was turned to the mirror and with her positioned in front of him the camera couldn't record the movement of their lips.

He spoke softly enough for the microphone not to pick up his words. "Help me."

Her look was forlorn. "How?"

"Help me get back to my pod."

He hesitated. Could he trust her? She'd said she wasn't associated with the SS, and he believed her. He'd smelled no lies on her, only pure, intoxicating woman. He made up his mind. Yes, he'd trust her.

"I can heal myself if I can get to my pod. There's an advanced medicine kit onboard."

Her eyes flittered in the direction of the mirror. "Where's your pod?"

"On the rooftop."

"There are many guards. They're armed."

"Get me out of that door, and I'll do the rest."

"You mean kill them?"

"Not if I don't have to."

She swallowed and looked away.

The mistake he made was to grip her chin and turn her face back to him. The minute his fingers touched her skin, he was lost. He could hear the pulse of the vein throbbing in her neck and smell the enticing cocktail of her blood. Try as he might, he couldn't break that spell. He was starving, not only for food or blood, but for a hunger he'd never experienced before, something food or drink wouldn't cure. He opened his legs wider and pulled her between them, forgetting for an Earth second that there were cruel men watching from behind a mirror. His only awareness was this woman and how her touch burned where she gripped his shoulders for balance.

"What are you doing?" she exclaimed on a panicked whisper.

"Keep still," he growled. "I won't hurt you."

He cupped her face and pulled her closer, close enough to drag his nose along the arch of her neck to her exposed shoulder. "I just want to smell you." He closed his eyes. "So good."

"Drako," she pushed on his shoulders. "Let me go."

"Just a taste," he pleaded, beside himself with desire.

With his nakedness, there was no hiding her effect on him. His cock turned painfully erect, and his balls drew tight. He was aroused, more than he'd ever been, but so was she. He could smell her feminine heat. Combined with the lure of her blood, it was more than he could bear. Flicking out his tongue, he traced the vein in her neck. She was the most delicious thing he'd tasted in his life.

"Drako." His name sounded like both an objection and a plea. "Don't touch me like this."

"Like how?"

"With your tongue."

"I may die without ever tasting you."

"Don't talk like this. You're not going to die."

At the rate his body was deteriorating, his death was a given. She was a medical professional. She should know.

He dropped his hands from her face to her hips, holding her in place to run his tongue over her shoulder. He felt her shiver between his palms.

"You like this," he said, triumph beating with the darkest of passions in his chest.

"Don't."

"Why?"

"They're watching."

"They can't see. I'm blocking the view."

"Not like this."

"Like what?" he said against the juncture of her neck and shoulder.

"You should stop."

When the faint smell of regret infused with her arousal, he almost did, but he was beyond reason. "I can't. All I see when I close my eyes is that wet uniform clinging to your body." His eyes pierced hers. "All I smell," he slipped his hand from her hip to cup between her legs, "is how wet you are."

A small gasp escaped her delicate throat. Her eyes grew large as he pulled her onto his lap, making her straddle him. Agent Pete and his cronies might storm through that door any minute, but he was willing to risk his life for a kiss.

"Let me taste you," he begged against her lips. "Just once."

Emotions played in her eyes. The mix was so complex he could barely distinguish the smell of her guilt from her fear, but the dominant fragrance was still desire. He brushed the thick plait of hair over her shoulder, exposing the milky flesh. Winding the braid around his hand just like he'd fantasized, he pulled it down gently to tilt up her head, holding her exactly where he wanted her.

"Open your lips for me," he instructed.

They remained tightly shut. He didn't miss the tremble of her mouth or the way her knees clutched him harder.

"Don't be afraid," he whispered.

Just one taste, and then he'd let her go. He'd escape, heal his injuries, and get a signal to Krina. She'd carry on with her noble profession and life, forgetting about the prisoner whose injuries she'd treated, but he needed to take this part of her with him, because he already knew he'd never forget her gentleness, goodness, or the way her heat surrounded him and made him dizzy.

Slowly, her body relaxed in his hold. With a small nod, she gave her consent. He didn't wait. He sealed his lips over hers, tracing the seam with his tongue. Her essence exploded in his senses, rendering him mindless. He was unable to think. He could only feel as heat travelled through his mouth down his spine, boiling his body from the inside out until his cock was about to blow. He delved deeper, thrusting his tongue into her mouth to be rewarded with a whimper. The sound was undiluted need. In a nanosecond, the sparks that sizzled under his skin combusted into flames. He sucked at her lips and tongue with all the hunger he felt, needing to feed on more than her desire. He wanted her very sentiments, the true ones that came from the heart. He needed to feed on her soul. He wanted to own it as much as he wanted to claim her body and keep it all to himself. The fire consumed him until there was only passion in its crudest form. Gnawing lust compelled him to tear his lips from hers, drag them down the column of her throat and open his jaw wide.

Before he realized what he was doing, the sharp points of his incisors pierced her skin. Placed on exactly the right mark, they sunk into the vein that had teased and beckoned him with its life essence from the first moment he'd laid eyes on her. Taste erupted on his tongue, overriding every other sense, including the distressed female cry that came from somewhere far-off. The universe fell away as pleasure detonated through his cells with the force of an earthquake. He sucked deep and swallowed and repeated the action. Somewhere in what was left of his cognizant mind, alarm bells rang, but he couldn't stop himself. He was drowning in the taste. Couldn't get enough. Just a sip. One more. So good. The pleasure so great it was painful. Yesss. He shivered with insatiate lust.

He only came back to himself when several arms jerked him from the woman in his lap. Growling like a beast, he swatted them away like flies, ready to kill to stop them from touching her, until he saw her lying pale and motionless on the floor.

No! Damnation.

They were trying to protect her. From *him*. He flew forward with a cry loud enough to tear the sky in two, trying to get to her, but Pete pushed a rifle in his face.

"Stay back."

A guard was kneeling next to her, slapping her face.

"Get your hands off her," he gritted out.

"What did you do to her?" Pete asked with a baffled expression.

Frik bent over her, studying her neck. He straightened with a boisterous laugh. "He bit her. He fucking bit her."

"What?" Pete looked between Drako and Ilse.

"He drained her," Frik said, still laughing. "Like a vampire."

Gripping his head, Drako turned in a circle. What had he done?

He'd never intended for it to go this far. He can't even remember exactly what had happened, except for the irresistible compulsion to bite down and swallow. After the first taste, he couldn't stop.

If he'd taken too much blood, he could heal her. He just needed to get to his pod.

He pushed forward. "Let me see her."

"You," Pete pointed the gun at him, "stay in your corner."

"He's a lunatic," Frik said, his voice carrying a measure of awe.

If anything, Drako only hated himself for the perverse admiration his act evoked in a bloodthirsty man like Frik.

"Chain him," Pete instructed a guard.

Too shaken and overcome with concern, Drako didn't fight as they dragged him back to the wall and shackled him. They splashed water on Ilse's cheeks and lifted her feet in the air. They pinched her nose shut and blew air through her mouth. They massaged her heart. When none of that worked, the guard kneeling next to her gave Pete a small shake of his head. "We need to call an ambulance."

"We can't." Frik pointed at her neck. "We can't explain that kind of wound."

"He's right," Pete said with resignation.

The guard abandoned his efforts and climbed to his feet.

"Help her," Drako said through gritted teeth.

They spared him a fleeting glance.

Pete dragged a hand over his head. "Shit. We'll have to think of a cover-up."

"Drug overdose?" Frik offered.

"No history of drug abuse. I checked her file before we hired her. It'll look too suspicious."

"Car accident, maybe."

Drako was about to pull the chains from the wall when she stirred. It was a slight movement, but she'd definitely whimpered. Her eyes shot open, taking in the room with a frown, as if she couldn't place where she was.

"Fuck," Frik said. "I thought she'd flat-lined."

She touched her neck and flinched. "What happened?"

"Ilse," Drako said, commanding her attention, wanting to apologize, explain, *what* he didn't know, but it was too late, she was already focused on Pete who helped her into a sitting position and said, "Nothing. Nothing happened. You fainted."

She glanced at Drako with knowledge in her eyes, but she didn't say anything.

"Do you need a moment?" Pete asked.

"I'm fine."

Pete offered her a hand and helped her up. She stumbled a step, and he grabbed her shoulders to steady her. A sound akin to a roar tore from Drako's chest at the sight of the other man's hands on her body. *Mine*, his whole being screamed.

"Are you sure you're okay?" Pete asked.

"Just a bit dizzy," she said. "It must be low blood sugar."

"Sure," Frik said with a snicker.

Pete gave him a hard look before turning his attention back on Ilse. "Do you need to drink or eat something?"

"No thanks. I'm good." She straightened her sweater, not meeting Drako's eyes.

"We'll continue this tomorrow." Pete turned to Frik. "Take Ilse home."

The pleasure of earlier made space for a hollowness in Drako's chest when she walked from the room. What in the stars of Krina had just happened? Had he almost killed the woman who dominated his thoughts and desires? The Krina leaders wouldn't be happy. Self-defense was one thing, but claiming to be a vegan and then sucking a woman dry like a vampire didn't make sense. It filled him with self-loath and disgust. He'd endangered her life to feed his lust. For that alone he deserved to die.

8

When Frik dropped Ilse off at home, she rushed inside and locked the door. Her body shook from head to toe. What had happened? One minute Drako was kissing her, making her drown in desire, and the next there was a sharp pain, stars exploding in her vision, and then she woke up on the floor. Hurrying to the mirror on the foyer wall, she studied her neck. There were two small wounds the size an injection would leave, and the flesh around them was red and puffy. Was he some kind of vampire? She pressed a shaky hand to her neck. Her skin was hot and clammy.

Not believing in overreacting or coming to hasty conclusions, she pushed the disconcerting emotions aside to first take care of her physical needs. She needed to calm down so that she could think clearly.

After a shower and one of her emergency stock TV-dinners, she made a cup of chamomile tea and sipped it on the back porch. It was close to eleven. She had to be up at three in the morning to start her shift at four, but there was no way she would be able to sleep. She needed to reflect on what had transpired tonight. Drako had said he wouldn't hurt her. Had he? Could she still trust him? Was her instinct about him wrong? Could he be the bad man Pete had painted? No, she couldn't believe that. Whatever had transpired had happened in the heat of the moment. It hadn't been premeditated. There had been an instance of pain, but she'd blacked out before it had gotten intense. If Drako's kind indeed had vampiric tendencies, the fact that the agents were starving him didn't help. Or was she trying to justify his behavior because she needed to believe he was good? If the men hadn't stopped him, would he have killed her? She supposed she would never know.

It only strengthened one notion. Drako didn't belong here. They had no right to keep him, or worse, kill him. The only honorable option was helping him to get home. If she was honest, she'd admit that her motivation wasn't purely logical or even moral. She didn't want him to die. She couldn't bear the thought. It was the part of her deeply connected to her emotions. Compassion. Yes, that was all it was.

Her decision made, she spent the night tossing and turning until a plan shaped in her mind. It was childish and risky, she'd go as far as to say immature, but she wasn't a mastermind criminal, and she didn't have time to become one. She needed her ducks in a row before her shift came to an end and an agent would be waiting to take her to Drako. At three, she got dressed, tying a scarf around her neck to hide the marks.

When she arrived at the hospital, she went straight to Caitlin's office. Caitlin wouldn't be in until noon. Guilt hammered in her ribs as she took the spare key from under the drawer where it was taped. They'd come up with the hiding place together after the last batch of medicine had been stolen. Her heart beat more loudly than her soles on the floor as she made her way to the depot. The depot staff worked normal hours, from eight to five. The security guard who kept watch knew her well.

He smiled when she approached. "Hey, Ilse. Whatsup?"

"Busy shift. The new nurse forgot to put in our order for insulin, again. I'm going to take some on loan. I'll get Caitlin to sign it off when she comes in."

He clicked his tongue. "Can't trust the young ones. You should give her flack about it."

"She'll learn." She smiled sweetly, holding her breath as he opened the door.

Once inside, she acted quickly. She grabbed a bottle of Lorazepam Intensol, emptied half of the tablets into her pocket, and snatched the insulin on her way out.

She presented it to the guard with the appropriate form. "Here you go."

As he studied the form and the medicine to make sure the information matched, she prayed he wouldn't search her. Searching had become standard procedure after the thefts, but she counted on their long acquaintance and his trust.

She almost exhaled audibly with relief when he waved her through. "All clear. Have a nice day."

The rest of the day dragged by. Caitlin commented on how pale she looked, but Ilse crossed her fingers behind her back and said she was coming down with a stomach bug and should take a few days for the virus to pass so that she didn't spread it to the staff and patients. She felt physically sick for leaving Caitlin in the lurch with a lie, going home early to put her imperfect plan in motion. If it didn't work, she was screwed. If it worked, it was going to change her life, but she couldn't see another way. She couldn't sit back and play accomplice to a horrible crime.

At a nearby mall, she bought hair dye and a new mobile phone. She packed it with some snacks, bottled water, her passport, and clothes in a travel bag, which she left in her trunk. Then she drove to Newtown and parked in front of Moyo, a popular tourist restaurant. From there, she caught a taxi home.

She spent the rest of the afternoon baking. When Frik came for her after four, he sniffed appreciatively as she opened the door.

Presenting him with the tray of chocolate-fudge cupcakes dripping with icing, she gave him a big smile, trying not to vomit with her own deception. "This is to say thank you for saving me yesterday."

He dragged his tongue over his teeth, giving her an once-over. "I didn't save you."

"You all did. Who knows what would've happened if you hadn't rushed in when you did?"

"Dunno." His gaze dropped to her breasts. "Looked like you enjoyed it."

"Maybe." She faked another smile. "Sometimes, I get carried away."

"Do you, now?" He reached out, tracing her cleavage. "Would you like to go out for drinks later tonight?"

She swallowed her revulsion. It took all her willpower not to punch him in the face. "Sure."

"Better get going, then. The sooner we start, the sooner we'll be finished." He took the tray, battling a bit with his casted wrist, and inclined his head toward the car. "Get inside, sweet tits. After you've done your magic on that freak, I'm going to show you how a real man fucks."

She bit her tongue to stop herself from replying. Frik deposited the cakes on the backseat before getting in beside her. She shifted as close to the door as she could get. It didn't stop him from putting his hand on her thigh.

"Tonight is Drako's last chance," he said, starting the engine.

She turned in her seat to face him. "What do you mean?"

"If he doesn't *deliver*, you'll never have to lay eyes on him again."

The air squeezed from her lungs. "What will happen to him?"

"We'll send him to Research."

Dear God, was there no end to the man's cruelty? "If he delivers?"

"Well, then you've got your work cut out for you." He winked.

At the building where they kept Drako, Frik marched her down the corridor with his arm around her shoulders as if he owned her while she carried the tray of cupcakes. Pete lifted an eyebrow when they approached, his gaze flickering between her and Frik.

"What's this?" he asked.

"Cupcakes," Frik replied.

She doubted Pete had been referring to the confectionary. More likely to their intimate stance, but she didn't reply.

Two of the guards stepped closer, their interest piqued.

"These are for all of you," she said, depositing it on a table in the hallway stacked with an urn, instant coffee, and Styrofoam cups. "It's to say thank you for yesterday."

"That was hardly necessary," Pete said.

Her heart threatened to explode from her chest with every lie that spilled from her mouth. If they didn't believe her, or one of them didn't eat the cake, she was dead.

She shrugged, hoping she appeared nonchalant and not as nervous as she felt. "You don't have to eat them if you're on a diet."

"I'm not on one," one of the guards said, grabbing a cupcake and peeling off the paper. He ate half of it with one bite, humming his approval. "This is delicious."

"Thanks," she said, repressing the urge to bite her nails. "Glad you like it." She'd been concerned that the copious amounts of sugar, chocolate, and caramel fudge wouldn't mask the bitter aftertaste of the tranquilizer.

"Are you ready to try again?" Pete asked. "This time, I'm not unchaining that bastard. There's no telling what he'll do when his hands come free."

"I only have one request." She didn't have to act apprehensive. That part came naturally. "Leave the door open. If anything happens, I want to know I can get out immediately."

"Nothing is going to happen. If he had the strength to break the chains, he would've done so by now. We used reinforced titanium."

"Still, I'd feel safer if the door was open."

"Fair enough. I supposed yesterday was traumatic." Pete nodded at Frik. "Take her inside."

To her dismay, Frik didn't let go of her while he ushered her inside. On the contrary, he seemed to make a big display of touching her.

Drako lifted his head when they entered. His eyes didn't turn to the beautiful golden color she'd gotten used to, but to dirty copper. He first looked at the scarf tied around her neck, and then at her shoulder where Frik's hand rested. Fury radiated from him as Frik hugged her tighter and kissed her on the mouth.

"See you later, sweet tits." He pressed his lips to her ear and said loud enough for Drako to hear, "I'm going to fuck your pussy so sore you'll remember me for weeks."

Inwardly, she winced, but she had no choice but to offer Frik something that resembled an agreeable smile.

At the gesture, the chains restricting Drako's arms pulled tight.

"Do your thing, baby." Frik took a sample flask from the gurney and pressed it into her hand. "Tonight I want to see his cock ejaculate. This jar better be full when I come back for you. We're not paying you a million for nothing." Frik slapped her ass and walked from the room, leaving the door open.

Alone in the room with Drako, she lifted her gaze to receive the full blow of his scorn.

His eyes narrowed, watching her with a predator's intensity as she neared. "You said you weren't taken."

"I said I wasn't married," she said for the benefit of the microphone and the agents who were watching.

He uttered a wry laugh. "You also said you weren't associated with them. No wonder I couldn't smell your lie." His lips thinned. "I should've asked if you *worked* for them. Are you even a real nurse?"

Frik appeared in the door, a stun gun in his good hand. "If he's giving you trouble, I can teach him some manners, show him how we behave on this planet."

"It's okay," she said, glancing nervously over her shoulder at Frik. "I just need some privacy without you hovering in the door."

The agent touched his crotch, adjusting a hard-on. "Get on with it, then. I'll enjoy the show. I may even jack off while watching."

She cringed. When Frik disappeared, she stared at up Drako with what she hoped looked like an apology. Not moving her eyes from his, she ran her fingers gently up his thigh.

He bunched his jaw and ground his teeth, but his cock was already stirring.

"You're a good person," he said. "You don't have to do this."

"I'm not good," she said, thinking about the tranquilizer she'd stolen from the hospital, the pills in her bag she'd bought from the black market, and the lies she'd spun to Caitlin.

"You are," he insisted, his gaze already changing from that clouded coppery tone to gold.

She dragged her fingers closer to his crotch, regretting it but unable to prevent the sparks that tingled in her fingers at the feel of his skin. "Why would you say that?"

"*They*," he spat the word out, his tone bitter, "asked *what* I was. You were the only one who asked *who* I was."

Her fingers reached his scrotum. She caressed the soft skin until his balls contracted and pulled up into his body. His cock grew so hard it pressed flat against his abdomen, reaching way past his navel.

"Don't do it," he said, staring down at her with a mixture of anger and lust.

Had the agents eaten the cakes? How long would it take before the drug took effect? How long could she hold this off?

Frik's voice boomed through the microphone. "The bastard is as hard as he's going to get. Get on with it, already, unless you want a hand. I'm more than willing to help."

There was no turning back, now. If she didn't go through with it, the agents would see right through her. This was their only chance.

She wrapped her hand around his girth and squeezed. He made a hissing sound. Leaving the flask on the floor, she caressed his length. She had to use both hands to encircle him completely. A deeper groan escaped his chest.

"If you do this," he said through clenched teeth, "I'm dead. I don't believe that's what you really want."

She dropped to her knees. Sliding her palm over the crest and down, she lubricated his shaft with his pre-cum.

"Zut." Closing his eyes, he leaned his head against the wall and exhaled heavily.

At the next stroke, his thighs bunched, his knees bending as far as the chains allowed. He fought his arousal, cursing and gnashing his teeth, but it was no use. He breathed harder with every stroke. When she dragged her tongue over the slit in the smooth head, he jerked his head down to watch her with a molten look. She folded her lips around him, taking as much as she could, stroking the underside with her tongue. The groan he uttered almost sounded painful. He was keeping perfectly still, flattening his ass against the wall, his gaze glued to the wicked work of her lips. His grunts turned louder. He grew thicker in her mouth, more than what she could handle, but she relaxed her jaw and moved her hands faster.

Perspiration glimmered on his golden skin. She ached to rub against him, naked. Her body reacted to his, her underwear growing damp. Her pussy was swollen, and her clit throbbed with aching need. His nostrils flared as he took in every move, every second of her forced seduction.

"Ilse." He forced out her name, his face distorted in something that seemed closer to pain than pleasure.

Hearing her name on his lips sounded so exotic, so darkly sensual and needy she couldn't help the moan that sprouted from deep in her throat. The minute the sound escaped, he snapped. His hips went from motionless to rocking into her mouth, taking her lips with shallow strokes. Suddenly, despite the constraints, the roles were reversed. It was no longer she who was in control, but him. His pace quickened, his hips pivoting with harder thrusts.

"Zuuuut," he gritted out, the word laced with need.

It was agonizing. She knew, because that same need reflected in her core. Forgetting they had an audience, she barely resisted the urge to touch herself. She couldn't think straight while he was pumping into her mouth with distorted pleasure etched on his face and certainly not while his taste evoked a deep satisfaction and a warped desire to swallow him.

Almost too late, she remembered the reason for doing this. His cock jerked and his ass bunched. She pulled back, letting him slip from her mouth, eliciting a deep growl that tore from his chest. Reaching for the flask, she aimed it at his slit. His protest was only verbal, because he was still pumping himself into her hand, going faster than before. It didn't take long to finish him off or rather for him to use her hand to finish himself off. There was no confusion about who had taken charge. Powerful streams of semen squirted into the flask. He groaned as jet after jet erupted from his body until the flask was almost full. His climax lasted a long time. It seemed to hold his body in a vice, his abdomen scrunched into a slab of rock-hard muscle and his face contorted with ecstasy. With a last jerk of his cock, the vice gave way. He tilted back his head and sagged against the wall, his chest rising and falling with hard breaths.

Unwilling to let go just yet, she stroked him softly, drying him with her palms before planting a soft kiss on the crest. At the contact of her lips, he lifted his head wearily to look at her. His expression was too murky to read. There was that fuzzy light that came with the afterglow of a powerful release, but also something disturbing, a lot darker.

Vengeance.

She got to her feet, the flask with his semen in her hand. She capped it, nervously waiting for someone to charge through the door and call her bluff. She counted to five, and then to ten, but nothing happened.

Her body was going haywire, her nervous system scrambled with painful arousal, fear, guilt, regret, and the worst of all, the knowledge that she'd leave Drako with this impression of her. Swallowing hard, she moved to the door, her mask in place, just in case. Looking around it, her heart thumped heavily as she saw the agents lying on the floor, passed out. The drug had done its job.

"Ilse."

Drako's voice stilled her. She looked back over her shoulder at him and then wished she hadn't. There was enough hate in his gaze to burn her to ashes on the spot.

"This isn't over," he said.

She jerked back into motion, running into the hallway. Dropping the flask, she searched the guards' pockets for the key to the shackles, but it was nowhere to be found.

"Shit," she muttered under her breath, turning in a frantic circle.

Her gaze fell on the door that had to give access to the room with the mirror. She yanked on the handle, exhaling in relief when it opened. Inside, two guards were slumped over a desk. The mirror was a horrible real-life portrait in which Drako was displayed, hanging limply in his chains. The image of his shoulders slumping dejectedly would forever haunt her memory, but there was no time to linger on it. She looked around the room. There were screens and recording equipment, but she didn't stop to evaluate any of it. She jerked open the only drawer and went through it with distraught haste. Not there.

"Double shit."

Holding her breath, she grabbed hold of the first guard's hair and lifted his head. She managed to wiggle her hand into his shirt pocket, but felt nothing. She was about to go through his pants when a shadow fell through the door. Panic seized her. She froze.

The guard from the parking lot stood in the frame, his automatic rifle pointed at her. This was it. She was going to die.

His gaze ran over the men lying face-down on the desk. "What the hell is going on here?" He waved the weapon at her. "What have you done? I saw them on the monitor, passing out like flies."

She backed up to the wall. "Please. They were going to kill him." She motioned at the mirror with her head. "They're going to cut him up for research."

He glanced at the prisoner.

"You don't want to be responsible for his death. This is much bigger than national security. This is huge. I don't know which planet he's from, but he's much stronger than any human being. We don't want a whole planet of men like him to take revenge on us for torturing one of their kind to death."

"He killed an agent."

"He defended himself when they captured him. You know Pete's intentions aren't pure. You've seen what I did to Drako on the monitor. They want to sell his sperm to create an army of invincible soldiers. You know it's unethical. Please, you have to help me."

"What are you looking for?"

"The keys," she said with renewed hope. "We have to uncuff him."

An alarm sounded, followed by a flashing red light.

"Quickly," she begged. "The other guards must've seen the ones passed out in the corridor on the monitors. They'll be here soon."

He hesitated a moment, his gaze flying to the screen that showed several guards rushing up the stairs.

"Please," she said. "They're going to kill me."

"I don't know where the key is, but there's a lever that will release the cuffs in case the key's lost." He scurried toward the desk and pushed the guard lying over the computer keyboard aside. His finger hovered above a button on a control panel. "You better go. If they catch you, you're dead. I'll release him."

"What about you?"

"I'll say you did it and destroy the recording."

She backtracked to the door. "Thank you."

"Go!"

His finger came down on the button as she cleared the room.

9

Alarms blared. Red lights flashed. Drako was still recovering from the most explosive climax of his life and the bitter sentiments of betrayal when the shackles around his wrists and ankles sprang open with a click.

Free.

He stared at his hands and feet. Flexing his fingers, he took only a second to allow the blood-flow to return to his limbs before sprinting to the door. He didn't know what was happening, but he wasn't going to waste the opportunity.

As he rounded the corner, he skidded to a halt. A guard with a rifle stood in his path. The others lay on the floor, alive but motionless. Zut. He'd been caught before even making it out of his cell.

"Go," the guard shouted, motioning with the rifle to the door at the end of the corridor. "Get out of here!"

Surprised, he wasted no time in complying. He charged down the corridor and through the door, using the stairs to make his way to the rooftop. It was too dangerous to use the elevator. The guards could easily intercept it. The door to the warehouse was sealed, but it didn't take much force to pluck the electronic panel from the wall. The locking mechanism short-circuited, sparks flying everywhere. He dug his fingers between the wall and the door, pulling so hard he left indents in the metal. With a creak, the door gave, sliding open. Four baffled technicians in lab coats stared at him. They were unarmed. Their elimination wouldn't be necessary. They backed to the far side of the room. The ones not clutching clipboards to their chests threw their arms up in the air. Not sparing them a glance, he rushed to his pod and threw out the seat. From the storage space underneath, he retrieved the nano-healer. Then he scanned the pieces of the dismantled control board until he spotted the signal box. The monitors mounted on the walls showed armed guards hurrying up the stairs. From the distance remaining to the rooftop and the speed at which they were running, he judged it would take them less than five minutes to reach the warehouse. Already having determined an escape route during his previous visit up there, he didn't have to search. He activated the self-destruction button lodged in the front of the pod that would disintegrate it into nothingness, doing away with every piece of evidence, including the parts on the floor.

With the nano-healer and signal box clutched in his hands, he aimed for the windows. Running at full speed, he projected his body through the partially intact glass. What was left of it broke with a splintering sound. In a few more strides, he reached the helicopter. He was clambering inside when the first guards cleared the stairs. His enhanced hearing picked up the excited blabbering of the technicians as they directed the men outside. Before they could make it to the hole in the window, he had the blades spinning. A bullet tore through the air as he lifted off. Before a second could hit the craft, he tipped it sideways and angled down, using the buildings as a shield.

It was a good thing he'd gone to the trouble of learning how to fly this ancient machine. It wasn't as easy as the simulators he'd practiced on, but after a few tosses and a downward spiral, he got the hang of it. Far out of the line of fire, he straightened the craft and lifted high above the buildings. He needed somewhere safe to land, somewhere where he could heal himself and fix the communication box to send a distress signal to Krina. He opted for south, heading away from the residential suburbs. It wouldn't be long before the SS had another flying craft, maybe one of their fighter jets, on his tail. Landing soon was the safer option.

He chose a cluster of mine dumps, the dilapidated state of the buildings indicating it was deserted, the gold depleted. When he saw no movement on the ground, he set the helicopter down between two dumps the size of small mountains. To win time, he'd have to conceal the helicopter. After glancing around, he pulled a ripped plastic shade awning from the side of one of the buildings and covered the craft. The entrance to the mine was sealed, but he easily kicked it down. Taking shelter in the dusty tunnel, he started to work.

Escape had a sweet taste, but the bitterness of Ilse's betrayal wouldn't leave his mouth or heart. She was with Frik. The thought of her being that bastard human's *mate* was too much to handle. The sight of the agent's hands on her had torn him up inside. It was like a thousand knives slicing through his insides, a million times worse than all the electric shocks he'd endured at Ilse's lover's hands. To add to the insult, she'd covered up Drako's marks on her neck. The sight of that cloth hiding his claim had chaffed his gut. It was as if she was ashamed of them. He'd trusted her, but she was no different than her government men who'd captured him.

Something Pete had said yesterday had stuck in his mind. In the commotion that had followed after Drako had bitten Ilse, he hadn't registered it immediately, but his subconscious had known it was important enough to store in his memory. Pete had said he'd checked her file before *hiring* her. Then there was her expression when her hand had gripped his shaft right before she'd made him come, almost as if it was painful for her.

One by one, the puzzle pieces came together. Now it all made sense. Ilse had been hired to seduce him and steal his sperm, to deceive him in the worst possible way while toying not only with his manhood, but also with his heart. She'd teased him and tortured him with foreplay that hinted at so much more and left him with empty, unspoken promises and a hollow, aching need. He'd thought her kind. Gentle. Pure. She wasn't a nurse. She was an actress. A damn good one if she was able to mask her lies so well they smelled sweet, enticing. Addictive.

He simmered as he lifted the nano-healer from its protective cover and activated it before dragging the device over his wounds. He wouldn't forgive her easily. No, never. Forgetting her would be impossible. Her betrayal would forever torture his mind, but not as badly as her absence would torment his body. Bristling with renewed anger as the nano-healer did its work and the skin on his shoulder, hip, and shin closed up, the foreign bacteria dying, he took a vow in the depths of the golden sand of a place called Johannesburg on Earth. His escape from Earth might be pending, but he'd come back for her, and when he found her, he was going to finish what she'd started.

ILSE RAN down the stairs and out of the building. In her blind rush she tripped on the step down from the pavement into the road. Arms flailing, she righted her balance before hitting the tar and ran as fast as her legs could carry her without looking back. Damn. She should've had the foresight to steal Frik's car keys or least have learned how to hotwire an engine.

The noise of a helicopter pierced the air. She squinted up. The black SS craft lifted off the rooftop and dipped behind the old Absa Tower before disappearing from view. If the agents were airborne, their chances of spotting her were too good. She doubled her efforts, pumping her arms and putting an extra stretch in her legs until her lungs burned so much she thought they'd collapse. She sprinted toward Newtown with nothing but her keys and credit card in her pockets, praying to God she wouldn't be attacked by a thug on the way. It was only two kilometers, but a sharp pain stabbed in her side when she crossed over the old train tracks to what used to be the fresh food market, now converted into a theatre and glitzy tourist restaurant.

Heads turned as she neared the safe parking, but no one tried to stop her. She almost fell into her car, pulling off with screeching tires, but not yet feeling relief. She couldn't go home or back to the hospital, at least not for a while. Not only would Pete and his agents be looking for her the minute they woke and realized her deceit, but she might also have a vengeful extraterrestrial chasing her. She shivered as she recalled Drako's last words.

This isn't over.

Shaking the nagging fear, she concentrated on her breathing. If she was to survive, she had to be strong. This was her life, now, the choices she'd made. It would be tough, but at least she'd be able to live with herself. As she drove farther away from the horrid building with the broken windows, a dull ache set into her chest when she thought about Drako. On cue, the marks in her neck started to throb. Uninvited tears burned behind her eyes, but she blinked them away. Freedom was in sight. Before disappearing, she had a stop to make. She turned up the music to boost her spirits and took the highway to Alexandra.

She followed the GPS up to where the roads had been mapped, but after that the informal settlement was a maze of unrecorded streets. She had to stop three times to ask for directions. After getting lost twice, she pulled up at a makeshift shelter that consisted of a few corrugated iron sheets.

Mosa came outside to greet her. "I never thought you'd come."

Ilse took the medicine from her bag and handed it over. "Here you go."

"Thank you." The woman's weathered face pulled into a smile.

"You're most welcome."

"Will there be stock next month?"

"It's hard to say." She thought for a moment. "If you have any problems getting hold of the medicine, call me." She scribbled down her new number on an old grocery receipt and handed it over. "Here's my number."

Mosa took her arm and pulled her toward the shack. "You must stay for dinner."

"You're very kind, but I have to get going."

"I'm not sending you away on an empty stomach. Come inside."

Not wanting to be rude, Ilse allowed Mosa to escort her into the one-room dwelling. The ground floor was covered with cardboard. A pot simmered on a portable gas stove. In one corner stood a box that served as a table. Another held crockery and cooking utensils. A mattress was pushed up against the wall. Ilse's heart contracted at the poverty she witnessed. The bus and taxi fare to get to the hospital alone would cost half of the measly monthly pension the government paid.

Mosa dished up a bowl of soup and invited Ilse to sit down on an upturned beer case while she took the mattress. While they ate, Ilse asked about her family, and learned that the woman was a widow with four grown children who all worked in far-off towns. The last time she'd seen one of them had been over ten years.

After thanking her for the meal, Ilse took the money she had on her from her bag. "Please, you must take this."

Mosa pressed a hand on her heart. "Oh, no. You've already been much too kind."

"Please, I insist. I don't need it," she lied.

The woman reached for it hesitantly. "May God bless you."

She gave a nervous laugh. "I needed that blessing. It's getting late. I better go."

As she exited the shack, a hand folded around her wrist. She jumped with a start. A man dressed in a fitted shirt and fancy slacks looked her up and down.

"Who's this, Ouma?" he asked Mosa.

"A friend. Let her go."

The man didn't oblige. "What is she doing here?"

"She brought medicine. Now, let her go."

The man's eyes burned into hers. "Is it true?"

"Yes," Ilse said, swallowing.

His expression was skeptical. "Why?"

"The hospital was out of stock," Mosa said. "She's a nurse."

He narrowed his eyes. "And now there's stock?"

"Yes," Ilse lied.

One by one, he released his fingers. "All right." He nodded in agreement, but his small, knowing smile said he didn't believe her.

Mosa took her arm. "Don't mind Samuel. He's nothing but a small-time crook. All bark and no bite. I'd like to pay you for the medicine."

"Oh, no. That's not necessary."

"It's not the first time the hospital didn't have stock. I know how it works. You didn't get the pills from the hospital. You must've acquired the medicine elsewhere where it doesn't come free, or cheap, for that matter."

"You have your treatment. That's all that matters."

"Are you sure there's nothing I can give you in return? I don't have much money, but I can clean or cook."

Ilse squeezed Mosa's hand. "You're sweet, but I don't need anything."

"If there's ever something I can do for you, just say the word."

She shook Mosa's hand in greeting. "I'll keep that in mind."

Mosa saw her to her car and waved as she pulled off. Ilse watched the small, stooped-shouldered woman standing in front of a shack in her rearview mirror. There had to be more she could do for her and the countless others like her. A good start would be putting an end to the medicine smuggling and exposing the black market dealers. Maybe she could leak the information anonymously to the media. If the police were too corrupt to get involved, an international media scandal would force them to take action, unless they wanted to be exposed for their role in the crime.

Feeling slightly better after her decision, she drove to a hotel in Randburg and rented a room under a false name. She fell down on the bed, exhausted, and slept nine hours straight.

The sun was high when she finally woke from an empty stomach. She snacked on some of the supplies she'd packed, and then took care of her hair, dying it black before cutting it off just under her chin. The cut was a bit choppy, but it would do.

She stepped back to inspect her image in the mirror. She looked very different. If she could avoid using her identity card, no one would know who she was. Her money wouldn't last forever. She'd have to find odd jobs and keep on the move, not staying in one place for too long. In her current state of exhaustion, the idea alone was tiring. Maybe, one day, the dust would settle, and she could grow roots in an obscure little town where no one would ask questions about her past. Surely, Pete and Frik would eventually stop looking for her. They'd sweep all the evidence of their unorthodox experiment under the carpet, and no one would ever speak of it. Her beautiful alien would've gotten to his pod, healed his injuries, and found a way home. He'd look back on his experience with anger, but eventually his bad memories would fade until vengeance dwindled from a distant notion to forgotten. She'd carry on with her life, and all would be well. Yes, that was the hope she had to hold onto.

Despite having eaten, her lethargy wouldn't let her go. It was the after-effect of the stress and shock. What she needed was a warm drink and a few more hours of rest. She brewed a cup of tea from the complimentary hotel supply, switched on the television, and settled on the bed. Mindless channel hopping was a great way of relaxing. Maybe she'd catch up with an episode or two of her favorite series. It always made her forget about reality for a couple of hours. She was flicking through the channels, moving quickly through the news ones, when a familiar face caused her to pause. It couldn't be. She stared at her face, splayed on the screen, in shock. Depositing the teacup on the nightstand, she turned up the volume and sat up straight.

"A police investigation confirmed a nurse at the Johannesburg General Hospital to be responsible for the theft of over a billion rand's worth of medicine," the reporter said. "The disappearance of prescription drugs from government institutions is one of the country's biggest and most costly obstacles in providing health care. Thousands of state patients suffer annually due to the unavailability of medicinal drugs. Nurse Ilse Gouws is said to run a black market operation in Johannesburg, with possible ties to others in Cape Town, Durban, and Bloemfontein." The camera zoomed in on a photo of her in her nurse's uniform that had been taken during the inauguration of the new children's wing. "Police are offering a reward of five thousand rand to anyone with information about her whereabouts that will lead to her arrest. Nurse Gouws is Caucasian, one meter fifty-six, with blue eyes and blonde hair. The suspect is dangerous and should not be approached. Citizens with information should call Special Agent Pete Evans." A contact number for Pete ran over the bottom of the screen. "Nurse Gouws has last been seen in the vicinity of Newtown."

She sank back against the headboard in a haze, her hands shaking so badly she battled to press the off-button on the remote. This was bad. No, this was infinitely worse than any outcome she could've ever imagined. She'd been framed. The whole country was on the lookout for her. Pete would've been to the hospital to pose questions. Dear God. Was Caitlin all right? Would they have harassed her? Would they have believed her if she said she didn't know where Ilse was? Everyone at the hospital knew she and Caitlin were friends. She jumped from the bed, chewing her nail.

Please, please don't let anything happen to Caitlin.

Sick with worry and tension, she stared at the phone on the

bureau. Calling was risky, but she had to know. After another second's hesitation, her concern for her friend won over her fear for herself. Her insides twisting together, she dialed Caitlin's mobile number.

"Yes?" Caitlin answered in her usual, brusque manner, which indicated it was a busy shift.

"Hi," she said softly, not sure how to explain without endangering Caitlin's life. "It's me."

She didn't dare say her name. Caitlin would recognize her voice.

"Hi, Mom," Caitlin replied in a too-loud voice. "You caught me at a bad time. I'm really busy. I'll call you back tonight, okay?"

Shit. The agents were screening her calls or they'd tapped her phone.

"Okay," she said, the word a mere whisper.

The concern in Caitlin's voice was palpable. "Take care, all right?" She hung up without waiting for Ilse's greeting.

Ilse replaced the phone on the rest with trembling fingers. She had to leave. Now. The receptionist could've seen the broadcast and remembered she'd checked in. Others had seen her in the elevator as she'd made her way to her room. She threw her bag on the bed and dumped her clothes inside. She rushed through the room like a mad person, grabbing toiletries from the bathroom and yanking her jacket from the closet. Zipping the bag closed, she considered her options, of which she seemed to have less and less. For the life of her, she couldn't think up a plan. Where could she go? Where could she hide? She needed to lose the car. The cops would be searching for her number plates.

With her heart beating so loud it was painful to breathe, she opened the door and looked down the corridor. Empty. Aware of the security cameras, she slipped down the hallway, opting for the stairs that led to the parking. She dumped her bag in the trunk and left the hotel with no idea of where she was going.

10

The serving counter rotated with a selection of Drako's favorite dishes, but it wasn't the food that held his attention. It was the image of the blonde Earthling with the blue eyes in the hologram. The picture was so life-like it inspired both longing and wrath. Since the ship sent from Krina had rescued him, he couldn't think about anything––or rather, anyone––else. He couldn't eat or sleep. Like a cruel joke, her intoxicating attributes had stuck in his mind to haunt his senses. He could still smell her skin and taste her on his tongue. Every time he closed his eyes, he felt the way her soft body had molded around his. He could only obsess about the human female and how to get her back, which was why he'd called this meeting straight after he'd gone through a medical check-up and the debriefing of his crash.

"Hence," Altair, the commander in charge of the Krinar's displacement, continued, "you wouldn't advocate cohabitation with humans."

He spared another glance at the hologram, the picture making his chest ache. "I'd say peaceful coexistence is highly unlikely, but it requires further investigation."

Kahvissar, one of the highest-ranking diplomats in the Krina galaxy, turned to him. "The Elders have a high regard of your opinion. It will weigh heavy in their decision."

"He's still very young," Altair argued, "and the wisdom required in such a decision only comes with age."

"The decision isn't mine to make. Whether we allow the humans to exist or not is up to the Elders," Drako argued.

"You will vote against allowing them to live?" Altair queried.

"Yes," he said with hard determination. "My experience may have been brief, but from what I've seen, human nature is frivolous, deceitful, greedy, dishonest, and they possess no self-pride."

"Yet, you plead for this female's life," Kahvissar said, studying the hologram with a finger pressed to his lips.

"Yes." The word sounded harsh.

Kahvissar uttered a soft laugh. "Your female seems to be even more flawed than the crimes you've accounted to her." He swiped through the hologram images to the broadcast declaring her a black market medicine dealer.

Drako swallowed hard. He couldn't deny the accusation made sense. How else would she have gotten hold of medicine like antibiotics that weren't available from over the counter? The statistics were shocking. Billions of rands' worth of medicine was stolen each year. Only more proof of how unworthy these humans were of the Krinar's aid. *His* human. No matter what she'd done, he'd claimed her the minute he'd sunk his teeth into her skin. Who was he kidding? He'd claimed her the moment he'd gotten a whiff of her smell, even before he'd laid eyes on her.

"I understand your need for revenge," Altair said, "but it's not an honorable or valid reason to abduct an Earthling. Let her own kind deal with her. They'll catch up with her sooner or later."

His hackles rose. No one was going to deal with her but him. "It's not about revenge," he said. "I bit her. I drank her blood. She's in my veins." Suddenly tired, he sank back on his plank. "Literally."

"You have to be careful." Kahvissar got up and folded his hands behind his back. "Taking blood can easily turn into an addiction for both of you."

"I'm aware of the perils," he snapped.

The medical overseer had explained it to him in detail. It was a pity he hadn't explained it *before* Drako had been sent to Earth.

"I wouldn't mind a taste," Kahvissar said. "It sounds rather enticing."

"Give me permission to go back to Earth and bring the female to Krina," Drako said, "or at least to a Krina station."

"We can't allow such an exception," Altair replied, "not unless you claim her as your charl."

"No." Drako jumped to his feet. "She's not my charl." Not after what she'd done to him.

Kahvissar raised a brow. "What then? A harlot?"

"Call it what you want. She's mine, but I won't take her as my charl." Not the woman who'd betrayed him.

"Slavery has long since been abolished," Altair said.

His patience was wearing thin. "I don't want her as a slave."

"As what then?" Altair asked.

"A sexual partner."

"Ah." He sighed. "We can't give her indemnity under our law or save her from conviction by her kind unless she's a charl. It pains me, but if you're not interested in taking her as your charl, you're going to have to give her up."

Drako pushed to his feet. "I don't want her as a human mate. I just don't want her to die."

Kahvissar flicked through more of the retrieved satellite archive images until he got to the one of Ilse on her knees in front of Drako's naked body. He tilted his head. "Mind you, if you're looking for a willing suitor, I'm prepared to save her. I'll take her as my charl."

Drako closed his fist, killing the hologram. "I don't think so."

Altair sighed again, more deeply this time. "I'll tell you what.

We have two Earth months until the Elders gather to discuss the course of action. I'll grant you access to Earth for a month to make up your mind. You'll either return with the female as your charl, let someone else take her as charl, or she suffers whatever fate the Elders decide for her race. If her own kind catches up with her before then, so be it. She'll live by her laws and judgment."

"Deal," he said.

It was better than nothing. Maybe, in an Earth month he'd have worked her out of his system, and his persistent hard-on would abate. These violent feelings would've calmed enough for him to take a distance, to let Kahvissar be the one to save her.

"When you come back," Kahvissar said, "you will hand her over to me. I like her wild spirit, and her ... other talents."

He ground his teeth. The image of her with Kahvissar was somewhere he couldn't go, not even in his mind, but he'd meant it when he'd said he didn't want her dead.

"Fine," he said. "If she'll have you, you can take her as your charl."

"Deal," Kahvissar echoed, his smile broad.

THE FUEL TANK showed the car was near empty. Ilse had been driving around without direction, nearly going out of her mind with every minute that passed, knowing she was taking a risk being on the road but not having anywhere to go. She was circling the city when a sign indicated the northern highway was approaching. At long last, a plan formed in her mind. She took the highway and went off at Alexandra. With a good sense of direction, she easily found her way back to Mosa's home.

The old lady exited her shack when Ilse parked.

"I didn't expect another visit so soon," Mosa said with a toothless grin when Ilse got out of her car, "which is why I'm all the more happy for it." She wrinkled her nose. "What's up with the new hair?"

Guilt burned like acid in Ilse's chest. "I shouldn't be here, but I couldn't think of anywhere else to go."

The lines around Mosa's wise eyes crinkled. "You're in trouble."

"I need to lie low for a while."

"You came to the right place. If you want to disappear, there's nowhere better than Alexandra."

With the vastness of the informal settlement and the quick rate at which it changed, shacks being dismantled and new ones going up almost hourly, it was a maze for the police to search. On top of that, not many officers risked going into the suburb, knowing how easily people got knifed down in the streets, especially law enforcers for nothing more than sporting a badge.

"I'm sorry for putting you in this situation. If you can put me up just until I've made another plan, I'd be eternally grateful. I'll be out of your hair in a couple of days."

"Stay as long as you like. Come." Mosa pushed her toward the entrance of the shack. "You must be hungry. I'm making lunch."

"Don't put yourself out on my behalf." Ilse trudged along with heavy feet. "Pretend I'm not here."

Mosa threw back her head and laughed. "Are you joking? I'm not missing out on having company. No, we're going to eat, and then we're playing cards. I haven't had a rummy partner in ages."

Despite herself, Ilse smiled, following Mosa into the dark interior.

Stirring a pot on the gas stove, Mosa pointed at the box with crockery. "You can set the table. Make sure you use my best tableware."

She winked as Ilse pulled out the only two bowls and cups, the bowls cracked and the cups chipped. Ilse grinned at the humor. A little bit of the darkness in her soul lifted.

"After lunch," Mosa continued, "I'll get Samuel to bring us another mattress."

"I'm sorry to be so much trouble."

"No trouble at all. After the way you helped me, I'm glad you're giving me the chance to do something for you." She switched off the gas and poured soup into the bowls, setting one in front of Ilse. "Eat up." She gave another wink. "You'll need your strength to fetch our bath water."

Mosa was a kind and distracting hostess. Little by little, Ilse relaxed at her banter and anecdotes. After lunch, they set off to fetch water. The nearest tap with running water was a good five kilometer-walk. It took them more than an hour to make the round-trip with Mosa carrying a large container on her head without spilling a drop. Ilse had a harder time with the two five liter-containers. Ten kilos got heavy after five kilometers of walking, and not used to the chore, her fingers ached where she grasped the handles. While Ilse filled the water jug and heated the rest in a big pot for their bath, Mosa set off to find Samuel.

A long while later, Samuel and a man who introduced himself as Abel came walking up the dust road, carrying a mattress between them.

Walking up ahead, Mosa waved. She called from a distance, "I got you sheets and a blanket from the neighbor."

Ilse rushed forward to take Mosa's load. "I don't know how to thank you." She nodded her gratitude to the men.

Samuel left the mattress against the wall opposite Mosa's and came outside with his hands on his hips. He eyed Ilse's hair. "You're the woman from yesterday, the one who brought the medicine."

Damn. She'd hoped it would be a bit more challenging to recognize her.

Mosa waved Abel off with an impatient flick of her hand. When he was gone, she turned to Samuel. "She's my guest for a few days, and it'll be wise if you keep this to yourself and your mouth shut about the medicine."

He gave Ilse a look of contempt. "You mean she's hiding. That's the only reason why a woman with decent clothes and an expensive car would camp out in your shack."

Mosa pointed a finger at him. "Don't get cheeky. She's been good to me."

"Sure." He snorted. "She's got money." He motioned at the gold ring on her finger. "She should pay if she's going to lodge here."

"Leave it, Samuel," Mosa said angrily.

In an automatic reaction, Ilse placed a palm over her hand, hiding the ring. It had been her mom's.

"Why must the rich bitch stay for free?" he asked.

"Samuel," Mosa said in a chastising tone.

"He's right," Ilse said quickly. "Look, the ring has sentimental value, but if you help me sell my car I can pay for my board and give you commission."

Mosa shook her pepper-gray head. "Ilse, no."

"It's better this way," she said. "I need to get rid of it."

"Fifty percent," Samuel said.

"Fine." She couldn't sell it herself. Anything was better than nothing.

He held out a hand. "It's a deal. How much do you want for it?"

She shook his hand. "Whatever you can get."

"I'll come back tomorrow if I can find a buyer."

"Great. Thank you."

He spared Mosa a glance before sauntering down the road, kicking at a rock.

"Let's get dinner going," Mosa said, "and then you can tell me all about this trouble you're in."

"It's not that I don't trust you, but the less you know the better."

"I'm not going to talk to anyone, and no one is going to ask me questions. What does an old woman like me know, anyway? We're going to talk, and you're going to get this thing that's eating you and giving you wrinkles from all that frowning off your chest."

Ilse gave her a grateful smile. "I'm so glad I met you."

"So am I."

Inside, Mosa made coffee while Ilse explained what had happened at the risk of sounding crazy. She told her about buying the medicine from the black market dealer, the Krinar the SS had captured, helping him escape, and being framed by the SS. Mosa listened quietly until she'd finished, and then said, "You can't run from the government. Not forever."

"I know."

"Do you think the alien, this man called Drako, will come after you?"

"Maybe. I'm hoping he made it back home." She wiped her palms over her face. "I hope in a few weeks' time all of this will seem like just a very bad dream."

Mosa patted her hand. "I'm afraid that's wishful thinking. You need to get out of the country, go over the border."

"How? I'll be stopped by border control."

"I have some friends from Lesotho who work in the mines. They know how to get across the border undetected. I'll ask them to take you."

"They're working here illegally, you mean."

"Yes. I have family in Lesotho. They'll take you in. It'll give you time to work out something."

"I don't want to drag you into my mess."

"No one will suspect a thing. I'll get a message to my friends at the mine. One of them should be able to get leave for the weekend to take you to Lesotho."

Ilse took a shaky breath. "If Samuel manages to sell my car, you must keep my half."

"No," Mosa said with much determination. "You will need it. Maybe you can buy a fake passport and bus fare to Namibia, and start a new life there. This thing the SS did is terrible. They won't let it go. Imagine what trouble it'll cause for our government if it ever comes out. The whole world will be against us. Best-case scenario, there'll be sanctions against South Africa. Worst case, the SS will be accused of human rights violations. To ensure that doesn't happen, they won't stop hunting you until you're dead. You mustn't talk to anyone about this. Don't tell anyone what you've told me. Money makes good people commit horrendous crimes, and that reward on your head is as good a temptation as one can get."

"Don't I know that."

Mosa took their empty mugs and got to her feet. "Let's not talk about this, anymore. Even in Alexandra, the walls have ears." She carried the mugs to the dish that served as kitchen sink.

"I need to use a smartphone. Do you know anyone who'd let me use theirs?"

"What for?"

"To send an anonymous tip about the black market dealer to the media."

"I'll ask the man who'll call my friends at the mine if we can borrow his phone. Go ahead and wash up first. I'll go now to give you privacy."

Mosa lifted the cloth that served as door and left the shack. When the makeshift curtain fell back, Ilse filled the plastic bath with the water she'd heated and stripped her blouse. The day was hot. The walk to fetch water had been long and the road dusty. She'd feel better after cleaning up. She was reaching for the button of her jeans when the flap lifted and light streamed into the shack. She turned with a start. Samuel walked through the entrance, his stride urgent.

She pressed the blouse to her chest. "You should knock."

He laughed. "In case you haven't noticed, there's no door."

"Mosa's not here."

"I know."

"Did you come about the car? Have you found a buyer, already?"

"No." His fingers locked around her wrist. "I came for five thousand rand."

11

"How are you going to locate this woman?" Kahvissar asked. Drako paced the floor of the main flight deck. "Her government has a price on her head."

"Exactly. They'll find her before you do."

"Most communication on Earth works via satellite. It was easy enough to hack into every one floating in space."

"And?"

Drako placed his palms on the control counter, the frustration chafing not only his patience, but also his nerves. "There have been a lot of red flags raised, but all false alarms. Fake claims of having spotted her." He had to find his fugitive. If her own people did, she'd be convicted for her crime, and he didn't want her punished in a barbarous human way.

"It seems there's another flag now." Kahvissar leaned closer to the screen to read the information. "A call from Alexandra to your infamous Agent Evans."

Drako listened with half an ear. He'd accessed every record on Earth, from Ilse's address to her listed numbers, but there was no sign of her. She was on the run. He needed a different tactic. The minute he got his hands on Ilse, he was planting a tracker under her skin. He wasn't going to risk ever losing sight of her again.

"The man says he has the suspect detained," Kahvissar continued. "Would you like to watch the satellite feed?"

"Why not?" Drako replied listlessly.

All the claims to date had been false. He didn't expect this one to be different.

Kahvissar manipulated the controls, using the mobile number to pinpoint the caller's location before zooming in on the area. Drako stared at the planets that zipped past through the outlook window. They couldn't stay in orbit like this indefinitely. If the search didn't bring up any results, he'd have to risk moving among humans to conduct a hands-on investigation.

"I have a visual on the owner of that number," Kahvissar said. "He has a woman with him, but I don't think it's your Ilse."

Drako twirled around, all the nerve endings in his body buzzing to attention. Kahvissar had enlarged satellite images that showed a male and female walking down an alley between temporary constructions. The female's back was turned to them. She had shorter hair and the color was wrong. Yet, a spark of hope ignited in Drako's chest. At first glance, she didn't look like Ilse, but the curve of her hips, the tightness of her ample ass, and her height were exactly right. He leaned closer to the monitor, every muscle in his body going taut. More images from different satellites filled the screen until the human pair was shown from every angle. He held his breath as he fixed his attention on the one where he had a full frontal view. *Crute.* His fingers clenched on the counter. She'd changed her hair, but it was her. His human. At the sight of the man's hand around her upper arm, he suppressed a growl.

"Is it her?" Kahvissar asked.

"Yes," he hissed. "It's Ilse."

"How are you going to proceed?"

"I'm going to prepare my pod."

The technician had ensured him this time it would work. They'd adjusted the technology for the Earth's atmosphere. He shouldn't have any problems staying invisible or landing.

"What happens when you get to Earth? How will you maintain discretion?"

"I'm going to construct a dwelling."

"Using Krina technology?"

"Of course."

"And then?"

"After a month, I'll be back."

A grin spread over Kahvissar's face. "With my charl, I hope. I've always wanted an Earthling companion. I can't wait to taste her blood. If your turbulent emotions where the woman is concerned are anything to go by, she must be extraordinary."

Anger slithered up Drako's spine, although he had no reason to be upset with Kahvissar. Kahvissar was simply expressing his wishes. Still, the idea of Ilse in Kahvissar's hands evoked feelings of violence.

"I suggest you heed caution," Drako said, jealousy tainting his voice. "She may not want to be your charl."

"In that case, she's doomed."

Never. He'd never send her to doom. He couldn't forgive her betrayal, and he'd never trust her, but he didn't want her in prison, or worse, dead. He'd rather suffer the pain of giving her to someone else than having her life snuffed out.

Without further delay, he stalked to the launch pad where his new pod waited. Less than a Krina hour later, he landed on Earth, near the location where the man was holding Ilse prisoner. He'd chosen a patch of dirt the children used as a soccer field. There was no need to conceal his craft, as it was invisible to both the human and Krinar eye. He moved fast, too fast by Earth standards, but he didn't care. All that mattered was getting back the woman who was so small she could've been a toy. His deceitful, beautiful, false little doll.

The signal on his communication system indicated that Ilse's captor was keeping her in one of the box-sized structures that consisted of metal, plastic, and cardboard. He stopped in front of the dwelling, his breath chasing with a mixture of excitement and stress. The door was bolted from the inside. Voices reached him through the thin walls.

"Don't worry," a male voice said. "Frik will be here soon to collect his prize. I'm sure you're looking forward to seeing him. As for me, I'm looking forward to the five grand he's going to pay me. You turned out to be my good fortune."

Whoever had her was asking ransom from Frik. Darkness blurred his vision. She was still with that cruel Earthling. Tough luck, as the human saying went. She was going to miss Frik, and she'd better get used to it. Impatience ruling over common sense, he didn't think twice. With a flick of his hand, he swiped away the wall that contained the door. Fury raged in his chest at the sight that greeted him. Ilse was sitting on the floor, blindfolded, her feet and hands bound. A man pointed a gun at her. The man's eyes flared as the wall, which was nothing more than a metal sheet, fell into the house.

"What the fuck?" The man jumped to his feet, swinging the gun in Drako's direction.

A female shriek pierced the air, but he didn't stop to pay her attention. Not yet. Before the man knew what was happening, Drako had grabbed the gun and bent the barrel.

The man stared at the damage with wide eyes. "What the hell are you?"

A backhand shut the man up, sending him flying. He remained motionless where he fell. Drako bent down and felt his pulse. He was alive, although he didn't deserve to be, not for what he'd done to Ilse. Only then did he turn his attention to her. Her chest heaved. The vein that had seduced him and made him lose all reason fluttered frantically in her neck.

"Frik?" she asked in a high-pitched voice.

He clenched his jaw. No, it wasn't her lover boy. He didn't bother to answer. She'd find out soon enough. He took the auto-injector from his pocket and injected it into the muscle of her upper arm. In a second, her body went slack. Before her back hit the ground, he caught her, sweeping her up in his arms. She was small and light, her physical attributes a reminder of her fragility. He stepped over the unconscious man on the ground and chose the quiet roads to go back to his pod. Within seconds, they were air-born. He knew exactly where to construct her prison. At the deserted mine dumps, he touched down, ensuring the invisible feature remained activated. The safest point was the highest one.

With Ilse in his arms, Drako climbed to the top of the mine dump. Krina technology allowed him to construct a comfortable den in minutes. Like the pod, the den would be invisible to any eye. He entered inside with Ilse. The den had everything from an advanced kitchen to self-adjusting, controlled temperature. Stepping into the bedroom, he laid her down on the intelligent bed. He'd tasted her blood and kissed her lips, but he'd not seen her naked. He couldn't help taking his time in removing her clothes, item by item, appreciating every inch of her skin. Her breasts were round and soft with perfect little nipples. Her stomach quivered as he dipped his fingers under the waistband of her jeans to unfasten the button, as if she was aware of him even in her sleep. He dragged the pants over her hips, her soft skin sliding under his fingers. She was physically perfect and morally flawed, but she was his. At least for the month Altair had granted him. In a month, he'd feed on her body as often as his cock got hard. He'd cure the need in his loins and the lust in his veins. In thirty days, he'd get her and her enticing little body out of his system.

12

Life returned to Ilse's limbs, but not reality. She blinked, trying to clear her vision and the fog that clouded her mind. Her throat was dry, and her head pounded. Her skin itched. She tried to lift her hand to scratch her arm, but it wouldn't cooperate. Frowning, she strained her neck to take in her body and then gasped. Cold shivers ran down her spine. She was spread-eagled and bound to a bed. Naked.

Jerking on the ropes that held her hands and feet, she suppressed a sob.

Don't panic.

She inhaled deeply a couple of times.

Don't panic. Don't panic.

The tension only made her headache worse. What had happened? After calling Pete, Samuel had blindfolded and tied her up on Pete's instruction, who'd said Frik was on his way to get her. Then the wall of the shack had fallen down and someone had injected her with something that had knocked her out.

Where was she? She took stock of the room. It was unlike

anything she'd seen. The bed was circular, reflecting the domed ceiling. The mattress was so soft and comfortable it seemed to mold to her back. Everything was a clean, off-white color. Except for the bed, there were no other furnishings. Despite her resolution, panic gripped her. Who had taken her? What was he going to do to her?

The questions were still assaulting her mind when an opening appeared in the wall. Her mouth dropped open. What *was* this place? Then all of her disconcerting questions were answered in a frightening, shocking instant when an impossibly tall, muscled man stepped through the entrance.

Drako.

Her breath caught. Her heartbeat spiked, sending her pulse through the roof.

He gave her a lazy smile––the unfriendly kind––while advancing slowly to the bed. "You're awake."

He was taller than she remembered, or maybe he carried himself taller than what chains allowed. Slacks covered his legs, but his sleeveless T-shirt bared his shoulders. The wound was completely healed, not as much as a scar in sight. The improbability of a wound like that healing in such a way only made her anxiety climb.

She yanked on the restraints. "Let me go."

He stopped at the foot end. Like his smile, there was nothing friendly in his voice. "How does it feel, Ilse?"

She tried to swallow away the dryness of her throat, but there was no saliva to alleviate the sandpapery burn.

"How does what feel?" she croaked.

"To be so helpless?"

She concentrated on not choking on her tears. "What are you going to do to me?"

Ever so slowly, he leaned over the bed, placing his hands on either side of her hips. Catching his weight on his arms, he lowered his upper body between her legs. He held her eyes as he dipped his head, his lips close enough to touch her core. A full-body shiver ran over her.

Hot air from his lips scorched her sex as he spoke. "What do you think?"

Reflexively, she tried to close her legs, which only invited a cruel chuckle from him.

"Please," she whispered. "Don't."

"You're at *my* mercy, now," he said. "How does it feel, Ilse? Tell me."

"I'm sorry! I didn't have a choice."

"You're a liar," he said with a sneer. "Everything that came out of your mouth was false, except for this."

The way his eyes darkened from yellow to gold warned her of his intent. She thrashed in her constraints. God knew how many times she'd dreamt about his mouth on her, but not like this. Not for warped reasons.

"Drako, don't."

Ignoring her protest, he flicked out his tongue. Light like a feather, he drew the tip over her clit. She jerked at the contact. A flame of desire licked over her skin, instantly setting off a dull ache in the nub. Without giving her time to process the sensation, he pressed his tongue flat on her folds and licked her from top to bottom. What was supposed to be a protest came out as an embarrassingly needy whimper. Her thighs quivered as he repeated the action, dragging his tongue through her slit. Heat penetrated her pussy, making her shiver despite how frightened she was.

"Do you like that?" he asked with a humorless grin. "Or are you going to lie about it, too?"

Before she could reply, he lapped at her with two long strokes before clamping his teeth over her clit and licking the sensitive bundle of nerves like candy. This time, the flame spread like a wildfire through her body. Her breasts turned heavy and her nipples hard. Her folds throbbed with slick wetness coating them.

She bit down hard on her lip to prevent a moan from escaping. She wanted to look away from him, not wanting him to see the effect he had on her in her eyes, but he held her gaze with an unspoken demand. His expression was dark with lust, but above all with satisfaction, the angry kind that came with retribution. By responding to him, she was giving him exactly what he wanted. Revenge. Her helplessness to stop her reaction turned her fear into anger.

"You lied to me, too," she snapped.

Releasing her clit, he lifted his head a fraction. His eyes narrowed with a calculating look. "When did I ever tell you an untruth?"

"You said you wouldn't bite."

Some of the anger in his expression made way for guilt. "It wasn't supposed to happen." His gaze moved to her neck. "I would've used my technology to heal you and take away any discomfort, but I see the marks are already gone." He smiled coldly. "I suppose you're happy. At least you don't have to cover your neck in shame."

"What was that, anyway? Are you a vampire?"

"My species take pleasure from drinking blood, but only in small quantities."

"Oh, great. You take pleasure from our pain."

He flinched. "It wasn't supposed to be painful. If done during intercourse, you will have more pleasure than you've ever felt."

"I prefer not to have a repeat. It was horrible."

"It won't be next time," he insisted.

"I fainted, and when I woke I couldn't remember what had happened. No thanks. I'll skip."

He lifted another inch off her, his heat disappearing. "I went overboard, but that's because I was starving, and I didn't know all the facts. Next time, I'll have better control."

"Don't count on it. As I said, there won't be a next time."

"We'll see about that."

"You can't keep me here against my will."

"I already am."

"Untie me." She scowled at him. "Give me my clothes."

He laughed softly. "Sorry, little doll." He placed his palm on her stomach, making her skin contract. "This time, the roles are reversed. You'll stay naked, and I'll decide what to do with you."

He trailed his fingers over her mound to cup her sex. She was intensely aware of how wet she was from both arousal and his tongue.

"Is this what your government pays you for? To get wet for men?" He circled his thumb over her clit, dragging the pad through the discriminating evidence. "You're trained much better than the first whore they sent."

"I'm not a prostitute, and I'm not *trained* to get wet for *men*."

His smile was pure evil. "Only for me?"

"No." Damn. If he didn't stop touching her she was going to come. She bit the inside of her cheek hard.

He stopped rubbing her clit only to flick his index finger over the nub. It was a matter of seconds.

"I beg to differ," he said. "You're always wet when you're near me."

She pulled on the ropes in frustration. "I'm not."

Piercing her with his iron gaze, he abandoned her clit to drag his finger through her folds.

She wanted him to both stop and continue. Being so close to coming and needing the release with an intensity new to her was more than she could bear.

Triumphantly, he lifted his finger to her face. "See?" His eyes turned hard, mocking. "I guess you lied again."

"You're a bastard." She suppressed a sob of humiliation. "Go on. Just do it."

"Do what?"

"Do what I did to you so that I can get on with my life. That's what you want, isn't it? Revenge."

He pushed to his feet. The last of his warmth evaporated, leaving her cold. "Oh, but you're wrong, my little doll. It's not revenge I want."

"Then what?" she cried in frustration. "What do you want from me?"

His words were measured. "To finish what you've started."

A chill ran over her. "Y-you mean like oral sex?"

His smile turned thin. "I mean sex."

"S-sex? With you?" Her gaze slipped to the bulge in his pants. It would never work. It couldn't fit. Was it even possible between their species?

"Fornication, coupling, banging, fucking. Do you need me to quote more terms?"

"No," she whispered. "I get it." She took a deep breath, trying not to hyperventilate. "Are you going to rape me?"

He gave her a hard look. "I'm not like you."

Ouch. She guessed she deserved that. "I'm sorry, Drako. Really, I am. I wish you'd believe me."

He turned his back on her and walked to the opening in the wall.

"Wait!" She didn't want to be left here on her own with nothing but her frantic thoughts. "Just let me go. I won't tell anyone, I swear."

"You'll go when I'm ready to let you go and not a second before."

"If you think I'm going to have sex with you willingly, you're mistaken."

He chuckled. "Time will tell."

A heavier thought struck her. What if his motives were darker than punishment for her actions? She knew who and what he was. If he set her free, he had no guarantee she wouldn't talk.

She shuddered. "You're not going to let me go, are you?"

Emotions flickered across his face. "Maybe not."

There it was. The truth. She steeled herself with another shaky breath. She refused to show him her fear. "Sex isn't going to happen, so you may as well kill me now."

"I'm not going to kill you."

"Why did you take me, Drako? Are you going to turn me into some kind of sex slave?"

"No," he bit out.

"Then why keep me?"

"To save you."

"From what?"

"It's complicated."

"From what?" she insisted. "If you're not planning on letting me go, you may as well tell me."

"Fine." He took a step back to her. "You want the truth? The Krinar, my people, sent me on a mission to Earth. My goal was to determine if our species could live together in peace."

Please don't let it be what she was thinking. "You're going to invade our planet."

When he didn't answer, her worst suspicion was confirmed. "Oh, my God. It's true."

He gave her a guilty look. "Nothing is certain."

"You wanted to see how susceptible we are to sharing our habitat." She gasped. "You're going to tell your people to kill us."

"After what *your* people did to me, what else do you expect? To say you're kind and welcoming?"

"Not everyone is like Frik and Pete. I swear. Drako, you have to believe me. There are good people out there."

"Like you?" he scoffed.

She averted her gaze. "I'm sorry for what I did to you, but it was the only way to save you."

"Don't lie to me more than you already have!"

As if the sight of her made him sick, he looked away from her with a sneer and stomped through the opening in the wall. It closed behind him in a beautiful finality of velvet-soft cream.

She didn't know what was worse, being alone or with his

dooming presence. He didn't leave her for long. The wall reopened to reveal his imposing form. In his hand, he held a glass of water. With the worst of the shock being over, she took more time to study him. The fabric of his T-shirt and slacks were the same neutral color as the walls. It looked like linen, only softer. Everything seemed foreign. It made her throat close up with new alarm. What if he'd taken her to his planet?

She broke out in a cold sweat. "Where am I?"

He carried the glass to her. "Don't fret. You're still on Earth."

She exhaled in relief. He stopped at the side of the bed, looking down at her with a broody expression. Miraculously, the ropes around her wrists and ankles started untying all by themselves. They curled and pulled, a slow dance of magic, as if invisible hands were manipulating them.

She stared at them in wonder. "Am I hallucinating?"

"It's real," he said in a clipped tone. "Move your arms."

Obeying the order, she lifted an arm. He hadn't lied. "How did you do that?"

"Krina technology."

She pushed up on her elbows, but he placed a palm on her chest. "Slowly. You may be dizzy from the tranquilizer. Thirsty?"

She nodded.

He supported her neck and brought the glass to her lips. She drank until the glass was empty and licked the drop that ran over her lips.

"More?" he asked, following the movement of her tongue with his eyes.

"Please."

"Stay there."

He walked to the wall and disappeared through the opening, which this time didn't close. She strained her neck to see around the opening, but could discern nothing but bright light that streamed from the other room. He returned shortly with a jug of water, refilling the glass and helping her to drink.

"Thank you," she said when she'd had her fill.

"Water is free," he said, "since that's the one kindness you showed me, and so is the bathroom."

"Free?"

His gaze remained cold. "Everything else you have to pay for."

Her jaw dropped. "You want money?"

"No." That icy gaze settled on her breasts. "We'll negotiate terms."

Vividly, she imagined those terms. She swallowed back an insult. There was no point in provoking him. She'd pretend to go along with his game and use whatever freedom he gave her to find a way to escape. Since the bathroom was *free*, she'd take that.

"I'd like to have a shower." Every muscle in her body ached. She felt weak from the drug. A warm shower will make her feel better and help her gain back her strength.

"Through there." He indicated the opposite wall.

Another opening appeared, revealing a bathroom with white fittings.

"How do you do that?"

"How it works doesn't concern you." He took a few steps away from the bed, giving her space. "Do you need help?"

She gave him a cutting look. "Not from you. I'll manage."

His yellow eyes turned hard. "As you wish."

"Drako?"

"Yes?"

She wanted to thank him for saving her from Samuel, but since he only did it to kidnap her, she supposed gratitude wasn't in order. Instead, she asked, "How did you find me?"

"Technology."

"That doesn't concern me?"

"Exactly."

Before she'd blinked, he was gone, leaving the wall open behind him. If he wasn't moving like a flash, he was stalking like a graceful predator, a prowler that matched his bloodthirsty trait.

From the way her legs were shaking and sweat beaded on her forehead, the drug was still strong in her system. She ignored the nausea. She wouldn't be sick. Mind over matter. At least her body was hydrated. She sat up and swung her legs over the bed. Feeling dizzy, just as Drako had predicted, she got up slowly. The carpet was soft under her feet, the fibers massaging her soles. For a few seconds she stood still, enjoying the sensation. When she felt more stable, she made her way to the bathroom. Halfway there, her head started spinning. She reached for the wall, pushing one palm on the smooth surface and the other on her stomach. Inhaling deeply, she concentrated hard on not falling over or being sick all over Drako's magic carpet.

A blur of movement flashed in her peripheral vision, and then Drako was at her side. The speediness of his actions only added to her disorientation, making her feel more light-headed.

"Ilse." His hands fastened on her hips, burning like branding irons. "Come here."

He scooped her up in his arms, cradling her against his chest.

Acutely aware of her nakedness, she pushed at his chest. "I'm fine."

"Keep still," he chastised. "I told you you'd be unstable."

He carried her to the bathroom and lowered her onto a bench, which was strangely warm under her naked backside.

"Let me check you out." He swept his hands over her shoulders and down her arms. "Where does it ache?"

"My head." She touched her temple where pain was throbbing.

"The drug must've dehydrated you," he mused. "What else?"

"Just a bit of dizziness and nausea."

"You're shivering. Are you cold?"

"A little."

"You have a very susceptible nervous system to have such strong reactions. I'm sorry for the side-effects, but sedating you was the easiest way."

She couldn't keep the bitterness from her voice. "For you."

He ignored the comment. "Wait here."

"Where else am I going to go?"

He opened his mouth as if to say something, but shut it again. When he left the bathroom, she leaned against the cool wall, closing her eyes. As shivers continued to wrack her body, the wall seemed to adapt to her needs, turning warm. She had under-floor heating in her house, but she'd never experienced wall heating.

Drako's voice spoke next to her. "You'll be better in no time."

She opened her eyes. She hadn't heard him came back. The man really moved like a panther.

He cupped her neck. "Don't be afraid. This won't hurt."

In his hand, he held a flat device the size of credit card. As he pointed it at her skull, she pulled away.

"What is that? What are you going to do to me?"

His thumb brushed over the nape of her neck. "Relax. I'm going to make you better."

"Is this how you healed yourself?" She nodded at the device in his hand. "This is what you needed from your pod?"

He nodded. "Now, be quiet. Close your eyes."

Deep inside, she believed him. She didn't think he meant to harm her with the device. She tilted her head back, but kept her eyes open. Crouching in front of her, he angled the device at her forehead. A light came on and a red beam ran over her skin. The feeling was pleasantly tingling. In an instant, her headache disappeared. As he ran the beam over the length of her, every ache subsided. The fever vanished. The nausea made way for a healthy appetite. Every muscle relaxed. She felt revitalized, better than she'd felt in years.

"This is incredible," she whispered. "How does it work?"

"Advanced nanotechnology. Better?"

"Much."

He put the device aside. "You're welcome."

Instead of straightening, he remained crouched, bracing his hands on the bench on either side of her body. The color of his eyes intensified. A darker swirl of gold invaded the yellow until his irises were a deep, bronze color that seemed to come alive with fireworks. She couldn't look away. His gaze dropped to her lips. The way he stared at her mouth as if he wanted to eat her alive made her relive the memory of their kiss. It had been unlike any kiss she'd shared. The thought alone brought her body to life, her stomach contracting with flutters. She pushed her knees together. He didn't need to know how intense the reaction was he had on her. It would only put more power in his hands.

He abandoned his scrutiny of her lips to fix it on her breasts. His nostrils flared slightly. The direction in which his gaze shifted told her he knew exactly how turned on she was. She jumped when he gripped her knees and pulled her legs apart.

"What are you doing?"

All his attention honed in on the junction between her legs. He studied her unabashedly, just like he'd done the first day they'd met.

She strained against his hold. "Let go of me."

"You shave," he said, tilting his head to examine the landing strip trim.

"It's called waxing," she snapped. "Now let go. You're looking at me as if you're used to nothing."

He smirked. "Oh, I've seen my share of vaginas, but yours is beautiful. So pink and tight."

"I prefer not to discuss my vagina's attributes with you."

"I prefer to do a lot more than talking about how appealing your pussy is." He pressed his thumb on her clit. "You're wet." His eyes twinkled, easing some of the dark lust of earlier. "Again."

"It's a natural reaction. Don't flatter yourself."

"I forgot. You're trained to get like this."

"Go to hell."

He adjusted an impossibly huge hard-on, all the while massaging her clit in torturously slow circles. "I *am* in hell."

This was a dangerous situation. The more he touched her, the wetter she got. It was impossible not for him to notice the moisture leaking onto the insides of her legs.

"I want my clothes," she said defiantly.

"What are you willing to trade for them?"

"You're not seriously going to play this game, are you?"

"I'm always serious, little doll."

If she could've turned into a dragon, she would've spat fire. "You're infuriating. Stop touching me."

His thumb kept on teasing, working her into a tightly spun ball of desperate desire. Dear God, she was pathetic.

"An orgasm for your bra," he said without blinking.

"You're out of your mind."

"It's up to you." He shrugged. "You can cover up your cute tits and the way your nipples turn harder than pearls every time I touch you or have dinner with me naked."

Eating naked didn't sit right with her. Not while ogling her like he was, making a visual meal of her body. Surely, she could handle one orgasm. Maybe after two, he'd give her back her panties, too.

"Fine." She stopped fighting his hold and relaxed her legs, opening them wider. "Make it quick."

He clicked his tongue. "Rush the first time you're going to come for me? I don't think so."

Her cheeks heated, but she held her tongue.

Straightening, he offered her a hand. "Get up."

"Why?" She was starting to panic again. "What's wrong with here?"

"You're going to watch your reaction in case you're tempted to lie about it later and tell me you didn't enjoy it."

"I probably won't. This isn't a romantic situation. Just get it over with so I can have my clothes."

He didn't budge. He just stood there with his proffered hand.

Sighing, she put her palm in his and allowed him to pull her to her feet. He led her to a wall that opened to reveal a mirror. Out of nowhere, a plank appeared and drifted to them on the air, but she didn't have time to express her surprise, as the plank shifted neatly under her ass and rose, lifting her feet an inch off the floor. She yelped, grabbing at Drako's arms for support, but the floating seat was very stable and comfortable. Towering behind her, Drako dragged his hands over her shoulders down to her breasts. She gasped as he gripped her nipples and rolled them between his fingers. They extended further, turning even harder than before. The sensation echoed in her abdomen, sending more moisture to her folds. She caught Drako's gaze in the mirror as he studied her face.

"Look at you," he said. "Isn't that pretty?"

She had to admit there was something erotic about watching the wicked work of his hands. Her breasts appeared heavier. Her cheeks were flushed, and her lips parted. It was hard to deny the ecstasy when it was written all over her face.

"See how beautiful you look when you're wet?" he breathed in her neck.

He smoothed his hands over her stomach, down to her inner thighs. Dragging up his palms, he watched her intently as his fingers reached the apex of her sex. Lightly, he brushed them over her folds. She shivered. Her chest heaved with labored breaths.

"That's right, little doll. I want to make you shake with pleasure."

When he traced a finger over her slit, she closed her eyes and leaned her head back against his chest. A sharp pinch on her clit made her eyes fly open.

"Keep on watching," he said. "I want you to see what you look like when I make you come. There'll be no denying how much you enjoy it."

He was right. There was no denying the sensations that ran through her body as he gently slipped the first digit of a finger inside. Moaning, she bit her lip.

"You can be loud," he whispered, kissing her ear. "There's no one here to hear but me."

Turning his attention back to her face, he eased his finger all the way in. Her inner walls fluttered.

"More?" he said with an evil smile.

She managed nothing more than a whimper.

"That's my doll."

He kept on whispering words of praise and encouragement for her reaction as he started moving his finger, inviting louder moans and her body to writhe against his. With one arm clamped around her waist, he held her back to his stomach while adding another finger to the first. The fullness felt like heaven. She wanted to object and beg him not to stop at the same time. Already hot coils of pleasure twisted around her insides. She spread her legs wider, giving him better access.

"Yes, damn it all," he hissed, his gaze slipping from her face to where he was conducting his sensual assault on her most sensitive parts.

The pad of his thumb pressed down on her clit. She was going to come undone.

"Drako."

"Yes, Ilse. It's me taking your pleasure. Only me."

She cried out again as he picked up his pace, fucking her in all earnest with his fingers. She was helpless to prevent hot, intense pleasure from building inside her. She could stop it as little as she could stop the effect he had on her. Leaning back against him for support, she gave over to the sensations, allowing them to wrack her body. He flattened his hand, slapping the heel of his palm on her clit. Decadent, wet, spanking sounds filled the space. She gripped his hips, sinking her nails into the fabric of his slacks.

"Close?" he purred.

"Ah!" The brutality of the pleasure had her toes curl. "Mm-mm."

Withdrawing his fingers abruptly, he lifted her to her feet and pushed her upper body down with a hand between her shoulder blades. At the brusque change of positions, she caught her weight with her hands on a plank that had appeared miraculously in front of her. A protesting sound escaped her throat at the loss of his touch, but he filled her quickly and fully by pressing three fingers into her from behind. The stretch added a scorching pressure, making her need climb quicker. He fucked her hard, making her body sway to the hammering rhythm of his hand.

"Drako," she gasped.

His golden gaze lifted from her pussy to her face. "Show me."

She did. Her expression contorted in a mask of intense ecstasy as her orgasm detonated, pulling her muscles tight. Her thighs quivered, and her arms shook as spasms rippled through her body. Through it all, Drako kept up his harsh pace until she couldn't stand it any longer. Unable to do as much as speak coherently, she could only utter a protesting moan, shaking her head meekly. In the far-off corners of her mind, there was embarrassment for her distorted features and the way she chewed her lip to prevent herself from screaming, but she was too consumed with the sensations coursing through her body to give it another thought.

Only after several long seconds did Drako finally stop. Her body went limp. He had to catch her around the waist to prevent her from sliding to the floor. She was breathing hard, but so was he. The frightening length of his hard-on pressed against her backside as he leaned over her, pressing a kiss to her shoulder.

"Perfect," he whispered, "like I knew you'd be."

She hung her head in shame, unable to meet his eyes.

"Look at me," he demanded.

The uncompromising tone made her lift her head. His golden eyes met hers in the mirror.

"You loved that."

She didn't answer. She didn't have to. It had been obvious, but Drako wasn't content with her silence.

He gripped her hair into a ponytail, giving a soft yank. "Tell me you loved it."

She gave him a defiant stare. "You know I did."

"Tell me," he insisted.

He wasn't going to give up. He was much too obstinate when he had a point to prove. Anyway, her face had already given it all away. What difference would admitting it with words make?

"I liked it."

He chuckled. "That's rather mild. You can do better than that."

He was such an arrogant bastard. "Fine. I loved it. Happy?"

"How much?"

She wiggled in his grip, trying to duck under his arms, but he only tightened his hold.

"How much, little doll?"

"A lot!" She added angrily, "Wasn't that obvious?"

"Yes, but I like hearing you say it."

He released her hair to drag his fingers over her scalp. "How about that shower, now?"

God, yes. She needed to escape their intimacy.

He indicated the shower booth. "Take your time."

Thankfully, he left her to her privacy, giving her time not only for her grooming, but also to come to terms with what had happened. How easily she'd surrendered to him. He'd won this round, and she had a feeling he was going to win a whole lot more. With a weary sigh, she pushed away from the plank. Her body felt bruised in a good way, an experience she hadn't had in a long time. Dragging herself to the shower, she took a minute to figure out the controls. She was still trying to come to grips with an overly complicated system when the booth closed around her, encasing her in glass. She pressed on the walls in a fit of terror. The smaller the booth got, the faster her heart beat. She dragged her nails over the glass, looking for a seal or a door. When vapor poured from ventilation holes, obscuring her vision and preventing her from breathing, she lost it.

She hammered her fists on the walls. "Drako!"

She tried to suck in a breath, but there was only humidity. She was going to be smothered to death.

Choking, she banged her palm on the glass. "Drako! Please let me out."

The vapor became denser, the fog obscuring not only her sight, but also the little reason she was hanging onto.

Keep calm. Don't panic.

Repeating the mantra didn't help. Shit, she was going to black out. She focused on her breathing, clinging to reason, but then something inside of her snapped. She fought like an animal in a cage, clawing for freedom.

"Please, please," she panted. "No more. Please."

The vapor stopped, but she was too far gone to calm down. Hot air blew over her body and a sweet perfume filled the space. She just wanted out. Sobbing, she sunk to her knees, her palms pressed on the walls that kept on shrinking.

Drako came charging into the room, his eyes wild when they fixed on her. In a second, the capsule opened, cool air washing over her. She caught her weight on her hands, gulping air into her starved lungs.

"Crute." In a flash, he was in front of her, picking her up in his arms. "It's all right, Ilse. You're all right." He pressed her face to his broad chest and carried her to the bedroom. Sitting down on the edge, he cradled her in his lap. "Zut. What happened?"

"I-I…" She battled to speak through her violent sobs.

"Shh." He stroked her hair. "You're safe. I've got you."

He rocked her gently, his arms firm around her but not too tight. Eventually, his cooing words and soothing paid off, leaving her feeling slightly better and totally embarrassed.

"I'm sorry."

"Don't apologize." He kissed the top of her head. "Just tell me what happened."

"The shower. It closed in on me."

"Yes?" He frowned at her, as if her words were a mystery to him.

"I couldn't breathe. I was drowning."

"Of course you could breathe. You must've panicked. Do you suffer from a phobia?"

"I have a bit of claustrophobia."

"A bit?" He raised an eyebrow, a soft smile curving his lips.

"All right. A lot. I'm terrible with small spaces."

"I'm sorry, sweetheart." He nuzzled her temple. "I should've asked or at least have explained. It's an intelligent shower, but if it makes you nervous I'll construct something more traditional for you, something you're used to."

She stared at him in surprise. "You'd do that for me?" Wouldn't that be difficult and time-consuming? How long was he planning on playing this game?

"The idea isn't to torture you," he said, the warmth of his gaze chilling by several degrees. "I don't derive pleasure from making people suffer like humans do."

"Drako," she pleaded. "Not all humans are the same."

He dropped her to her feet. "In my experience, they are." All the distant coldness from earlier was back. He lifted her bra from the bed. The strap swinging from his finger, he held it to her. "Take it. You earned it."

Heat rose to her cheeks. Awkwardly, she reached for the scrap of lace. He didn't grant her privacy to fit it, but stood gawking while she pulled the straps over her shoulders and reached behind her back for the clasp. His eyes changed from winter-yellow to summer-gold as she adjusted the lace cups over her curves. Disconcertingly, the color didn't revert to its natural state, but remained dark and intense for the rest of the day.

THE JOKE WAS ON HIM. Drako watched Ilse as she padded through the living space, dressed only in that piece of lace that pushed her breasts higher and made the curves spill over the fabric. He longed to suck her hard little nipples into his mouth as much as he craved another taste of her blood, but he'd have to negotiate for it. His little doll wasn't giving anything freely. Not yet. Unlike her, he wouldn't take anything without her consent.

He crossed his arms as he studied her, frustration mounting with the painful hard-on in his pants. The combination of her naked pussy and ass with her concealed breasts was all the more enticing. The flesh hidden from him was a tease, one he barely resisted. He fought with every ounce of reserve he possessed not to flick that lace down and expose her perfect, bouncy flesh. She walked around the room, trailing her fingers over the wall, a frown marring her brow and her lip caught between her teeth. No doubt she was worrying her mind about where she was and when he'd set her free. Guilt stabbed at him, but he suppressed it. This wasn't a tenth of what she and her compatriots had made him suffer.

She turned to face him, and he couldn't help but stare at the delicate folds of her pussy the short-trimmed pubic hair didn't conceal. His mouth watered. His cock jerked in response. If he didn't find something to keep his hands busy, he was going to pounce on her, spread her legs, and devour her. Several times in a row.

The kitchen could prepare a meal on a voice command, but he opted for manual labor, needing the distraction. Turning his back on her, he took ingredients from the fridge. He'd stocked up with vegetables from her planet. She might need time to get accustomed to the Krina food types. Soon, the fragrance of a vegetable stir-fry filled the space. He smiled when she neared, sniffing with appreciation.

"Can I help?" she asked shyly.

"No." He pointed at a floating stool by the island counter. "You're my guest."

Her tone changed from uncertain to cocky. "Guest or prisoner?"

He only flashed her a smile over his shoulder. Sarcasm

wouldn't work on him. When the food was ready, he dished up a hearty portion and carried the plate to the counter. Dipping the fork into the food, he took a bite and hummed his approval. Scrumptious.

The way her eyes widened and she subconsciously licked her lips made his smile grow bigger.

He dabbed a napkin to his mouth. "Hungry?"

She should be. On cue, her stomach growled. She didn't ask, though. Pride, he guessed, prevented her.

He leaned his arms on the counter. "What are you prepared to give me in return for a bite?"

Her blue eyes flared. "You can't be serious."

"Why wouldn't I be? I took an orgasm for your bra. How about you let me make a meal out of your pussy in exchange for this meal?" He pushed the plate toward her. "Doesn't that sound fair?"

Her nostrils quivered. "Nothing about this is fair."

"Neither was locking me up, torturing me, and stealing my sperm."

She looked away.

He gripped her chin and forced her face back to his. "It's no big deal. All you have to do is hop onto this counter, spread your legs, and a lovely meal awaits you."

She jerked from his hold. "You're a bastard."

"So you've said."

"I hate you."

"Now, *that's* new."

"I suppose the feeling is mutual, or you wouldn't be doing this."

"Hate is a strong word for what I feel for you."

"What *do* you feel for me?"

"Let's just say the dominating feeling is lust."

"You hope to satisfy it by finishing what I started?"

"Exactly."

"Then you'll let me go?"

"When I'm satiated and I've worked you out of my system, yes."

"Why me?"

"You did something to me in that cell where your lover kept me."

"He's not my lover."

"Stop lying!"

"Drako, you have to listen to me."

"Stop." He held up his hands. "No more lies."

Her chest heaved with a sigh. "You want to bite me while having sex, don't you? Is this what you're referring to every time you talk about finishing what I've started? This is what it'll take for you to let me go?"

He couldn't deny it. There was no point in wasting words. Fear sparked in her eyes as the truth was laid on the table, naked and flawed. There was nothing right about what he wanted, except he couldn't turn his back on her and walk away.

"There's no need to rush into it," he said. "We'll take baby steps, starting with you spreading your legs for my tongue."

She gave him a hard look. "Is there no end to your perverseness?"

"Not where you're concerned, it seems."

Lust ate at his patience. His control was hanging by a thread. Hoping to speed her decision along, he lifted her onto the counter and pushed her legs apart. Her pussy lips were swollen and glistening with moisture.

"You're not put off by my proposal. Unlike your mouth, your pussy doesn't lie."

A war raged in her eyes. He could almost see the moral debate taking place in her mind. There was only one outcome to that debate. He had to have his way. He had to, if he wanted to walk away with his sanity intact. She'd eventually give him what he wanted, and they'd part ways. He'd go back to his life before the deceitful temptress had come along, once more finding peace in his work, and she'd go to live with Kahvissar. She'd be saved from both her government and the Krinar's conviction. Logically, it was the perfect solution. Only, that last part, the part where she lived with Kahvissar, chafed on his gut. It was a shard of glass under his skin. For now, he didn't pause to analyze it, not while her pussy was presented to him all wet and ready.

Placing a hand on her chest, he pushed her down gently, praying she wouldn't resist. "You can close your eyes, this time, if it'll be easier."

For two more seconds, her body remained tight, but then her muscles relaxed, and her legs fell open.

"Good little doll," he cooed, lightheaded from the rush of blood to his brain and cock.

He didn't waste time on making good on her non-verbal agreement while the offer lasted. His doll was temperamental. Who knew how long before her resistance flared again, denying him the sweet treat between her legs?

Her head was turned to the side, her eyes closed. He intended on keeping his open. He didn't want to miss a thing. Memories of the first and last time he tasted her pussy, mere hours ago, almost drove him to the brink of insanity. Gripping her thighs firmly, he laid into the meal. This time, there was no holding back. Dragging his tongue through her folds, he lapped up her sweetness. The taste made him heady. All for him. He speared into her heat, sucking and kissing until his cock was ready to blow. He latched onto her clit, pinching the nub with his lips while licking with his tongue. Beautiful sounds exploded from her chest. They told him what he wanted to hear, that she wanted this. Her back arched off the counter, pushing her deeper into his mouth. He growled against her flesh, sucking her harder and devouring her with his eyes. Crute, the way she reacted to him was hot. Her movements and whimpers increased in intensity and volume, telling him she was close.

"Yes," he said, digging his fingers into the soft flesh of her ass. "Come for me."

She came with a loud cry, her legs gripping his face. She wasn't going anywhere, but he held her ass firmly, making sure she couldn't escape his lips and tongue. When she fell limp, her body shaking in a tantalizing way that made him realize both what power he had and how vulnerable she was, he petted her clit with long, slow strokes of his tongue, prolonging the aftershocks that contracted her abdomen. Immense satisfaction burst through him, even more satisfying than the physical need this woman evoked in him. Slowly, he eased up, enjoying the way her chest rose and fell with violent breaths and how her skin glistened with perspiration. He was the cause of those reactions, and he wanted to be the last to evoke these feelings in her.

Opening her eyes, she stared at him with a drowsy look. Satisfied. He barely suppressed a grin. If she hadn't needed nourishment, he would've taken her straight back to bed for more *negotiations*.

"Come here." Pulling her into a sitting position, he kissed her long and hard.

The flavors of her mouth and body exploded in his senses. If he wasn't careful, he'd get addicted to her. With much effort, he broke the caress. Positioning her in his lap, he started feeding her, bite by bite, alternating them with sips of water, until she assured him she couldn't eat more. The simple act of taking care of her filled him with warmth he'd never felt before. Yes, Kahvissar had been right. Humans were addictive. Caution was most definitely advised.

He finished the rest of the food and set the empty plate aside. His thumb played over the tender flesh of her temple. "Would you like to rest or perhaps engage in an activity? You could read or watch a movie."

"Are you going to be here?"

"Of course. Where else would I go?"

"I don't know. I was hoping..."

"That I'd leave you alone so you can try and escape?"

Her cheeks flushed.

"Rest assured, little doll, there is no way out of here, so don't waste your energy." Since she wasn't going to decide, he'd make up her mind for her. At his voice command, a shelf in the wall slid open and a book drifted toward them. He caught it in mid-air.

"Here you go. Alien Invasion. According to your media, it's the latest bestseller." He winked. "I thought you might enjoy it."

She snatched the book from his hand. Obviously, she didn't find it funny. A plank drifted into position. Grudgingly, she sat down. Looking down at her, she made a beautiful sight. Her upper curves of her breasts were on display, as well as her toned stomach and legs. The only problem with the picture was that her legs were crossed.

"Open your legs for me, Ilse."

Her look was cutting. "Are we negotiating, again? What is it this time? You require a prime view in exchange for the book?"

"The book was a gift. It's simply a request."

"You're *asking*?"

"Yes. Nicely."

"Why? You've seen me enough times already."

"A thousand times and a million more will never be enough."

"I want the rest of my underwear."

"Your panties, you mean."

"Yes."

"Why?"

"The way you look at me makes me uncomfortable."

"I guess you better get used to it, because a lot of looking is going to happen between now and..." He couldn't finish the sentence, couldn't say, when I let you go.

She left the book on the plank and shifted to the edge. "I tell you what. How about if I do this?" Reaching for his slacks, she untied the drawstring. "Will this earn me the rest of my underwear?"

Crute, yes. He clenched his jaw, trying to contain his lust. "Are you doing the negotiation, now?"

"You bet."

She pushed the slacks over his hips, setting his cock free. It wasn't the first time she was doing this, but felt like a novelty, all the same. It didn't come without a tinge of bitterness at the memory of the last time she'd given him oral sex. Pushing the recollection aside, he focused on the present hotness of her mouth and the skillfulness of her tongue as she sucked him into oblivion and to places he was better off not going.

ILSE WAS LAYING on the plank with her head in Drako's lap, reading, or mostly pretending to read, while he played with her hair and worked on something embedded in his palm. The closest she came to a term for the astonishing phenomenon was a tablet or smartphone.

"Are you an explorer?" she asked.

He lowered his hand to look at her. "I suppose you could put it like that."

"Have you been on many explorations?"

"Some."

"To where?"

"Far-off galaxies."

"Were you searching for habitable planets?"

"I'm not a biologist or a geologist. I'm more of an adventurer."

"What does that mean?"

"I test new terrains for extreme sports."

"What about here? Why were you sent to Earth?"

"It was a once-off mission to investigate things of a more intangible nature."

"Like the probability of peaceful coexistence."

"Yes."

"When are you giving your decision about Earth to your leaders?"

"I already have."

A lump lodged in her throat. "What have they decided?"

"The Council is sitting in a month. They'll make their decision then."

"Based only on your feedback?"

"Based on various data they've captured over the centuries, and yes, on my feedback."

"Centuries?"

"Our species came from way back, long before we planted life on your planet."

"How does your lifespan compare to ours?"

"It doesn't."

"How old do you get on average? A hundred years? Give me an average figure."

"There's no figure."

She reflected for a while. The implication sounded ridiculous. "You live forever?"

That sounded silly. He was going to think her naïve. She couldn't help but laugh at herself.

He didn't return her laugh. He was dead serious when he said, "Yes."

She went completely still. Her heart skipped a beat. "You're not joking."

He threaded his fingers through her hair, seeming to sense her need for comfort at the shocking news.

"I'm not," he said gently.

"I see." She swallowed. "How old are you, Drako?"

"Not so old. Barely over five hundred Earth years."

She jerked into an upright position, dropping the book. "Five hundred years?"

He bent to retrieve the book. "That's what I said."

"Oh, my God." She pressed a hand to her chest.

"There are no diseases on Krina," he explained, "and as you've seen, we can heal any wound. It doesn't mean we're indestructible. Like any living creature, if injured critically, we will die."

"Wow, I don't know how to deal with what you've just told me."

"I can appreciate how overwhelming it must seem."

"Our planet can profit immensely from your technology. If you can cure any disease--"

"Your planet isn't ready." He pushed her aside and got to his feet. "In any event, it's not my or any Earthling's decision to make."

"Drako, you have to talk to them. If there is an advanced race out there, why would they refuse to help us?"

He stalked to the far end of the room. "Let's see, Ilse. Maybe because you don't deserve it?"

She jumped up, following him. "What happened to you was horrible and wrong. I'm the first one to admit it. Please believe me when I say I don't work for those agents. They brought me to you to treat your wounds."

He clenched his fists, the golden color of his eyes turning into frosted yellow. "You participated in their experiments. I know exactly how much they paid you. One million. Isn't that right?"

"I did what I had to do to win time. If not, they were going to kill you."

"Spare me your lies," he hissed. "I'm not interested in your false justifications."

Frustration turned into anger. "Just in my blood. That's why I'm really here. Admit it."

The one minute he was standing at the opposite side of the room, and the next he was in front of her. "Yes, I want your blood," he said through clenched teeth. "I never lied about it."

"If that's what it'll take to get me out of here, just do it." She tilted her head to the side, exposing her neck.

"You've got to be damn sure about this, my brave little doll, because once we go down that road, I won't be able to stop."

"Do it!"

He moved closer, his breath hot on her face. "So impatient. All you have to do is ask."

"What are you waiting for?" she challenged.

"Take off your underwear and lie down on the bed."

"You don't have to romance me," she snapped. "There's no need to pretend this is anything other than bloodthirsty lust. Just take me on the floor like the common whore you accuse me of being or better yet against the wall."

His laugh was cold. "It's got nothing to do with romance and everything with practicality. This is going to last for hours. I doubt you'll stand on your feet for that long, especially not with what I have in mind for your body."

A little of her bravery slipped. The last time he'd bitten her hadn't been pleasant. She hated the black void in her memory and not knowing what had happened. Not being in control or cognizant scared her.

"Not so brave, anymore?" he asked.

Screw him. "Fine. How do you want me?" she asked tartly. "On my back or on my knees?"

"We'll start on your back," he said, jerking the T-shirt over his head.

Her mouth turned dry at the sight of him. True, he was deliciously hard, a perfect male specimen, but he was also impossibly big. His weight alone could crush her. What if he drained her? There was no Frik or Pete to save her this time.

She wet her dry lips. "What if you go overboard?"

"However difficult it is to maintain control around you, I swear I won't take more than a sip. I've learned my lesson, and I'm wiser for it."

When he reached for his slacks, her courage almost failed her, while a shameful part of her wanted this. She wanted him inside of her as badly as she needed her freedom. The reason why she needed her freedom throbbed painfully inside her heart. She might not be the traitor he accused her of being, but she would be once she warned the world about the pending danger. How could she stand back and let Drako's leaders destroy mankind because of a few, twisted agents? If she didn't deserve his wrath now, she would later. She might as well take her punishment. The thought hurt more than she'd expected.

He dropped his slacks and stepped out of them. His erection jutted at her, inviting both desire and trepidation.

Taking his cock in his hand, he pumped twice. "If you want to back out, now is the time."

She lifted her chin. "I'm ready."

"Good." He scooped her into his arms. "So am I."

13

Drako carried Ilse with brisk strides to the bedroom, placing her in the middle of the mattress. The bed immediately started doing its magic, massaging her tense muscles.

His gaze was dark with hunger as he pushed open her legs and climbed between them. He hooked a finger under the elastic of her bra. There was a tearing sound, and then the bra fell open.

"Wait." She exhaled nervously. "If I give you this, you have to let me go."

His jaw bunched. "You want to be rid of me this badly?"

"I don't want to be your prisoner."

"Fine. You won't be."

"What about diseases or birth control?"

"Krinar don't have diseases, and I can't make babies with you."

"You're infertile?"

"Our sperm isn't compatible with humans."

"Oh. Shouldn't we talk about--"

She was going to say *conditions*, but he crushed his mouth to hers, spearing her lips with his tongue. He wasted no time in devouring her with a kiss. There was no going slow or practicing caution. He took her mouth as if he owned it, stroking the depths with his tongue and nipping at her lips with his sharp teeth. The kiss worked her into a frenzy of desire and wet need. Long before he abandoned her lips to attack her breasts, her ankles were locked around his ass, her pelvis grinding against his. With every move of her hips, he growled, the sound sending vibrations over her skin. He plumped up her breast in his hand and drew her nipple deep into his mouth. She yelped at the bite of pain. He let go with a pop, laving at the soreness he'd inflicted.

"So delicious," he muttered. "I can eat you all day."

She hoped he didn't mean it too literally, but she had no time to contemplate her uncertainty or fear, as his tongue trailed a path over her stomach to her pubic bone, making her shake with delicious anticipation. At the apex of her sex, he tortured her with soft licks and gentle suckles until she was begging for more.

"Please, Drako."

"I told you, all you have to do is ask."

"Let me come."

"That's exactly my intention."

His fingers played at her entrance. She moaned as he inserted one, then two, and three fingers.

"I want you," she panted. "Give me more than your hand."

"I have to prepare you," he said, biting down gently on her mound.

He brought her to the edge, but didn't give her enough to send her over. She was whimpering in frustration, but understanding that he was being considerate, making sure she was ready to take the size of his cock.

When the broad head of his cock finally prodded at her entrance, her courage almost failed her for a second time. No matter how wet she was or how long he'd fucked her with his fingers, she'd never truly be prepared. He shifted his hips, tilting them up until the crest of his shaft eased inside her. Her muscles resisted. It was too much. Too big. The stretch burned. Her inner walls clamped down on the invasion, trying to expel it.

"Relax," he said. "Let me in."

She pinched her eyes shut and tried to do as he'd asked, but it took great effort to slide his cock another inch inside her with still so many inches left. She shook her head. "It's not going to work."

"Shh." He kissed her lips. "We'll make it work. Look at me."

She opened her eyes to see the determination in his as well as tenderness and care. He was administering great control. She could see it in the way his arms shook and a muscle ticked in his jaw.

"Put your hands on my shoulders."

She only realized how badly she'd needed to hold onto him when she'd complied.

"That's my girl."

Holding his cock perfectly still, he rewarded her with a long, soft kiss. By the time he tore his lips from hers, her inner muscles had adjusted to his size, giving him easier entry.

"Zut. Yes."

He slipped deeper, the earlier pain returning.

"Drako, it hurts."

He gripped her nipple and pinched, drawing her attention to another part of her body. The sharp sensation wasn't all painful. It mixed with pleasure to make her ache with carnal need. Her clit throbbed, and her folds swelled more, turning her passage slicker.

"Ah, yes," he groaned. "Zut, you're tight."

His next words warned her his fucking was about to turn intense.

"I'm sorry, Ilse."

Drawing out until only the head of his cock was lodged inside her, he slammed back, tearing through sensitive tissue and setting every internal nerve ending on fire. She dug her nails into his shoulders.

Groaning, he kissed her lips. "The worst is over. I'm going to make this good for you. I promise."

She bit her lip. It was all she could do not to cry out. He was buried inside her as deep as he could go. Their groins were touching, his balls pressed flat against her ass. His hips jerked, but he gnashed his teeth and kept still. Holding his weight on one hand, he moved the other between their bodies, finding her clit. He wasn't gentle. He massaged the nub hard and fast, quickly bringing her back to the edge. Her channel relaxed, the inner muscles turning soft.

"That's it." He kissed her again and again. "You're doing so well."

"Drako." She clung to him, not wanting him to stop and frightened for him to carry on. Whatever was happening, it was going someplace deep and dark, someplace she'd never been.

"I've got you, little doll."

He did. She believed it. The minute she gave over to the knowledge, his kissing turned fierce. He pulled out and pounded into her. The force would've shifted her right across the bed had he not been holding onto her hip. His fingers dug into her flesh. He pumped into her, hard and fast. The ache in her core wasn't all pleasure. There was pain, too, but the good kind, the kind that would leave memorable bruises. Right now, she couldn't care. All she could care about was letting go, coming undone under and around him and marveling at his invasion, wishing him to take more.

"More," she whispered, giving voice to her desire.

His picked up his pace. Grabbing her wrists, he kissed first one then the other before placing them above her head.

"I love looking at you like this," he gritted out, "splayed out for me."

The air left her lungs every time he thrust his cock into her.

"Mine," he groaned. "Your very breath is mine."

She couldn't contest it, not when he owned the moment, her

ecstasy, and everything that came with it, which was going to be her orgasm, too, in the next few seconds.

"I'm…" She gasped for breath.

His voice was animalistic. "Now?"

Suddenly, his pace slowed. His kiss turned gentle. He dragged his lips along her jaw and down the column of her neck. Her body tightened as his teeth scraped over her skin. She turned rigid, bracing herself for the pain.

The sky exploded, and she was sucked into a vortex of excruciating pleasure. Her scream had to have torn into that universe of unbearable ecstasy, but nothing was coherent save for the orgasm that wouldn't let her go. On and on it went, dragging her deeper, making her come harder. In and out of that darkness she floated. Drako's grunts and cries of pleasure accompanied her at times, and at others there was only the buzzing in her ears. Always there were his arms around her, holding her safe.

When she thought she'd die from it, that she couldn't take more, she tried to protest, but her teeth chattered too much to speak. Trembles wracked her body.

"P-please make it stop."

She couldn't be sure, but she thought that begging voice belonged to her. The one who answered was the master of her pleasure, the owner of her fate.

"It's a long night, still. Hold on for me, little doll. I'm not done with you, yet."

———

LIGHT INFILTRATED THE ROOM. It was artificial, but Drako thought it better to maintain light during the natural Earth day and darkness during the night. It would mess less with Ilse's metabolism and brain patterns. He looked down at the woman who slept with her head on his chest, her thigh thrown over his groin. His dick grew hard. Last night was indescribable. In his lifespan he'd had his fill of sexual partners, but it had never been like this, both stroking a deep physical and emotional need. It was as if this human woman was made for him. If anything, last night had only stoked his desire. He'd never get enough. A dark thought dowsed the pleasurable afterglow that relaxed not only his body, but also his mind. He'd promised to let her go. How could he do that after last night? She'd leave an aching hole in his chest.

Unable to resist the temptation, he pulled the sheet down her body, only to still.

"Zut," he muttered.

His heart picked up with an uneven beat, his throat pulling tight. Fury at himself coiled through his stomach, twisting his gut into a knot. Bruises in the shape of fingerprints marked her neck, back, hip, and thigh. There were blue marks on her slender wrist. He'd reminded himself to be gentle with her, remembering how easily he'd pulled a man three times her size apart. Seething with self-directed anger, he eased out from under her. The fact she didn't stir only concerned him more. She had to be exhausted. Standing over the bed, he stared at her body. If this was what she looked like on the outside, she had to have bruises on the inside.

A voice command brought the nano-healer to him. It was best he fixed her before she woke to this battered state. She'd never trust him again, if he even deserved her trust. With the task done, he left her to rest while he took care of breakfast and fabricating a new bra for the one he'd destroyed last night.

The chickpea omelet was just about done when she walked into the kitchen, the sheet draped around her body. She gave him a shy but glowing smile.

"Hey."

"Hi." He left the spatula on the counter to wrap his arms around her, inhaling the fragrance of her skin. He watched her closely. "How do you feel?"

"Good." Her cheeks turned a pretty pink. "Great, actually."

Inwardly, he sighed with relief. "What do you remember from last night?"

"Almost everything. Although, I think I blacked out, again."

He brushed a stray strand of hair from her cheek. "You did." Kissing her gently, he teased her tongue with the tip of his, enjoying her taste. Food. She needed to eat. With much difficulty, he set her aside.

She averted her eyes, toying with the edge of the sheet. "You said you'd let me go."

The notion stabbed him right in the heart. He put two steps between them.

"You should eat." He served the omelet on a plate and put it in front of her. "After last night, you need fuel."

A smile flirted with her lips. "There's no negotiation this time?"

"No." The word came out harshly. "Our game is over."

"Wow." Something like hurt flashed in her eyes. "You sure got over it fast."

"We made a deal. I stick to my promises."

"All right," she said slowly. "So, you *will* let me go?"

"Yes. Just not now. Eat up."

"Wait. What? What do you mean *not just now?*"

"Our time together isn't up, yet."

"You didn't mention a timeframe last night."

"You didn't ask."

"Don't throw technicalities in my face. We made a deal. You said you'd honor it."

"I will." He added, "When the time is right."

"When might that be?"

"Sooner than you think, but maybe not quite as soon as you hope."

"Stop being vague."

"Enough! I don't want to talk about it any longer. If it's the biting that concerns you, you needn't be. I won't take your blood again."

She almost seemed dejected. "I thought you liked it."

"I more than liked it. Loved it doesn't even come close to describing it. I guess adored would be as close as I could come in your human language. That's the problem. It's too damn good. If we do it too often, both of us will become addicted."

The delicate skin of her neck rippled as she swallowed. "I see."

"Eat now. Your food is getting cold."

"What about you?"

"I don't need to feed or sleep as often as you." With that, he stalked from the room.

While Ilse ate in the kitchen, Drako paced the living space. The idea of setting her free had him on edge more than he'd ever imagined. It turned him into an animal who wanted to protect his territory. He didn't enjoy the primal feelings. It made him nothing but barbaric. He was still sifting through his emotions, trying to force logic into the equation––yes, letting her go to Kahvissar made perfect sense, but it didn't mean he liked it––when she reentered the room, still wearing his bed sheet. She looked like she was walking on eggs.

"Thank you," she said softly. "The breakfast was delicious. I didn't realize how starved I was."

Just like that, he melted. His heart softened. "You're welcome."

He lifted the new bra and panties he'd made with the Krina technology from the table and offered it to her.

"For me?" She reached for the undergarments tentatively.

"To replace the one I destroyed yesterday."

"Oh. Thanks."

"Is there anything else you would like?"

Her look was hopeful. "Anything?"

"Yes, anything."

"A dress?" She bit her lip, staring at him in expectation.

Ah, zut. How can he deny her anything when she looked so gorgeous and so damn vulnerable? "Sure. Go ahead and use the bathroom. Your dress will be ready when you're done."

She hesitated, not heading for the door.

"What is it, little doll?" He needed her to know she could ask him anything. He didn't want her to be scared of him or doubt that he'd grant any reasonable request.

"Um, what you do want in return for the dress?"

"Nothing."

Her eyes grew large, the blue set off by her new, shiny black hair. "You were serious when you said the game's over. What has changed?"

"You've earned everything you want. You deserve anything you may wish for."

"Because of last night?"

Because he was tired of playing this game. He didn't want to punish her, any longer. He just wanted to be with her and forget the past and the future for a few days. He wanted whatever she was willing to give freely, not by manipulation or negotiation.

He nodded in the direction of the bathroom. "Go have your shower. I've changed the system to one you're used to, one that will stress you less."

She clutched the underwear to her chest. "When did you have time to do that?"

"While you were sleeping this morning."

"You remodeled a bathroom in a morning?"

"Enough of the questions. Go before I change my mind."

Her smell was much too tantalizing. He'd only just repaired her. He didn't want to tear her, again.

For once, she obeyed immediately and without question. She scurried away, leaving him impossibly hard and hopelessly frustrated.

When she got back to the lounge, a dress waited for her on one of the floating planks. She reached out to touch it, but probably thought the better of it, because she retracted her hand and looked at him instead. "May I?"

"Go ahead. It's for you."

His chest warmed with that familiar feeling he was fast getting used to at the sight of her obvious pleasure.

"It's so soft," she exclaimed.

"Try it on," he said with a smile.

Arms crossed, he stood watching her, taking joy in the simple act.

She pulled the dress over her head and turned in a circle. "How do I look?"

Perfect. Gorgeous. "It suits you."

He uttered a voice command, and the wall opened to expose a mirror. Hurrying to it, she studied herself, turning from left to right. The dress scooped low over her back. The high neck in the front emphasized the perfect shape of her breasts. The way the fabric fell softly over her hips to flare out to her knees highlighted the narrowness of her waist and the pert roundness of her ass.

She turned back to face him. "May I keep it on?"

"As you like. No more rules apply."

"You really meant it."

There was a bite to his words he couldn't help. "I never say anything I don't mean."

He immediately regretted it when a veil dropped over her expression and she averted her eyes. Trust him to spoil a perfect moment. In a desperate effort to rewind to the comfortable zone they'd just been in, he blurted, "Would you like to sit with me?"

"Sit with you?"

"Yes."

"And do what?"

"What do you mean *do what*?"

"We can't just sit."

"Why not?"

She sighed. "Never mind."

"What do you do when you sit?"

"I never do nothing. There's always too little time. I catch up with messages or emails, or I balance my checkbook."

"What do you do to relax?"

"I read a book or watch a movie."

He sat down on the plank and patted the space next to him. "Then we'll watch a movie."

"You're serious?"

"Why wouldn't I be?"

"It's just… I can't remember the last time I sat next to someone and watched a movie."

"What do you like?"

Taking a seat close to him, she grinned. "Romantic movies."

He grimaced. "I already don't like the sound of it."

At his command, the wall opened to expose a flat screen. A list of the latest movie releases showed on the screen.

"Choose something," he said.

After she'd made her choice, he pulled her close to him, holding her at his side. Right now, there was nowhere else in the galaxy he'd rather be.

IT SEEMED strange for the big, dangerous Krinar to cuddle with her, but Ilse reveled in his nearness and heat. Despite the situation, she started to relax. She ached for something other than his lust, something deeper. Something off-limits, because this couldn't go further than physical. They had no future. Soon, he'd set her free, and she'd have to warn the authorities about the Krinar's intentions, unless she could convince Drako otherwise and make him change his one-sided opinion of mankind. Thinking about it made her chest constrict painfully. She wouldn't think about it now, not when his arm came around her and he pushed her head down on his shoulder. Not while the moment was perfect.

Halfway into the movie, she dozed off. When Drako woke her with a gentle kiss, she rubbed her eyes.

"Sorry, I must've been more tired than I thought."

His gaze was concerned. "You didn't get much sleep last night. I wouldn't have woken you, but I have business to take care of. Why don't you go back to bed?"

"You're leaving?"

"I'll be back before you know it."

There was a warning in his voice, one she couldn't ignore.

Not wanting to break their comfortable spell, she said, "Did you really watch the rest of the movie all by yourself?"

His expression softened. "I was watching you."

The way he looked at her made her cheeks flush with a pleasant heat.

"Why do your human men offer their women gemstones?" he asked.

He was referring to a scene from the movie where the man gave his girlfriend a diamond ring.

"It's a symbol of affection. If a man loves a woman, he sometimes buys her a gift to express his feelings. It works both ways. A woman will buy a man something she hopes will please him. A ring symbolizes a bond that you promise to love that person and share your life with him."

"When you give a woman a ring, do you always *make love?*"

He uttered the expression carefully, as if he'd committed it to memory.

"It's not a requirement, but the physical act is a demonstration of love."

He seemed to ponder her words so seriously she couldn't help but smile. "Is it different on Krina?"

"We have a life-long bond with our partners, but we don't use jewelry as symbolism." He got to his feet, pulling her with him. "Go rest. I'll be back before lunch."

He didn't leave until she was in the bedroom. The minute he was gone, she went around the room, searching for an exit or a control to open the panel, but there was nothing. She only had access to the bathroom. Sighing in frustration, she sank down onto the bed. If only she could contact Caitlin and Mosa to make sure they were all right and to tell them not to worry about her.

———

DRAKO FLEW his pod to the Krinar station midway between Earth and Krina. The ship was manned with technicians, engineers, and researchers who oversaw interplanetary integration. On board was also Ehle, their expert in human behavior. Having requested an audience, Drako made his way straight to the behavioral scientist's office.

She greeted him with a friendly smile when he entered. "It's good to see you, Drako. I'm sorry about your recent misfortune on Earth."

He shrugged. "I survived."

"Still, such an experience must leave a mark."

He lifted his arms. "As you can see, I'm as good as new."

She came from around her desk, offering him a wise smile. "The most damaging are the marks we don't see."

"I'm not here to talk about the scars of my soul," he said wryly.

She indicated two visitors' planks facing a floating table. "If not to talk about your traumatic experience, why are you here?"

"I need information." He took a seat opposite her.

"About what?"

"About human behavior."

"Ah. What is it you'd like to know?"

"Can human nature change, or are characteristics and personality traits genetic?"

"Some traits are genetic, and others stem from learned behavior. Genetic ones are biologically programmed in the DNA and part and parcel of the human. To try and change such a trait would be stressful and even damaging to the human psyche. It would be like forcing an introvert to be sociable. Not only would the natural introvert find the forced situation stressful, but his psychological health could also suffer if others make him feel that his nature is unacceptable or unlikable. Such psychological stress, if prolonged, could result in detrimental physical damage, such as depression and even cardiac disease. Learned behavior can be changed, but it is a long and difficult process. Why do you ask?"

"Say for example a human is deceitful, could that change?"

"It depends on many factors, including personal motivation, role models, external factors, and mental health."

"Could you reprogram human DNA to remove the negative trait?"

"Impossible. There are too many variables and influencing factors. Some traits may be a combination of both learned and inherited behavior. I'm afraid tampering with their DNA can't alter human personality. Maybe before conception, but certainly not after birth." Crossing her legs, she gave him a piercing look. "Why are you so interested in this subject? You're an adventurer, not a psychologist."

He looked toward the window through which the planet of Earth was visible. "I met someone, a human, and I have strong … emotions … for her, but she betrayed me."

"I see." Her voice filled with compassion. "I couldn't say if she could change. Each individual is unique. There are no guarantees. Like any living creature's, human nature is complicated." She continued softly, "Would you trust a Krinar who betrayed you?"

"No," he said with regret. "I could never trust a Krinar if he deceived me."

"Then you have the answer you came for."

"Yes." He got to his feet, a heavy feeling settling in his heart. "I guess you're right. I thank you for your time."

"Go well, Drako. I hope to see you soon, again."

Unable to speak, he nodded his greeting and made his way to the door.

"Drako?"

He turned back to face the scientist.

"We can learn to trust again if that trust is earned."

"It's a noble concept, but I'm not that forgiving."

"I guess that's *your* inherited nature," she said with a smile. "Or maybe it's a part of you that could change."

He doubted it. This one cut too deep. It was ironic that it had to be the first woman he'd fallen in love with.

Thoughts mulled in his mind as he piloted his pod to Earth. Maybe he couldn't trust his human doll, but he could enjoy the last few days with her. The memories would be all he'd have. If she went to Kahvissar as his charl, he'd never be able to face his friend again. It would slice his heart open to see them together. The day he delivered her, he'd sign up for the explorations of new adventure terrains uncountable light-years away from Earth, to the farthest corners that posed the most danger. For now, though, he was on his way to Ilse. There was no point in tormenting himself with a future that would do the job all by itself.

An idea occurred to him as Johannesburg came into view. On impulse, he issued a voice command, requesting the system to show him a map of vendors in the proximity of his temporary dwelling.

Choosing the biggest one, he ventured south and landed next to a lake near the Bruma Market. Making his way through the market, he inspected the stalls that sold everything from garments to gadgets. At a jewelry stand, he paused to inspect the items on offer.

"Can I help you?" a woman asked.

She uttered a gasp when Drako looked up to meet her eyes. Pressing a hand over her heart, she exclaimed, "What in God's name are you?"

"An alien," he said drily. He hated that term, but it was the one all humans understood.

She stared at him for a moment, and then broke out into laughter. "Ha ha, very funny. You almost got me. You must be with the theatre group performing in the amphitheater. I have to say, you've got your role cut out for you. Nice contact lenses. Are you looking for something specific?"

"A gift." He looked over the earrings and bracelets pinned to a board. "For a woman."

"What's your relation, if I may ask?"

He frowned. "Why? Does it matter?"

"Why, yes. You wouldn't give your mother the same gift you'd give your girlfriend, now, would you?"

He tested the word on his tongue. "Girlfriend."

Taking it as his answer, the woman pushed a glass case filled with rings toward him. "In that case, I'd suggest something more intimate."

There were rings in gold and silver with every color stone in the galaxy. The choice was overwhelming. He leaned closer to inspect them. He wanted exactly the right one for Ilse.

"What is her birthstone?" the woman asked.

He gave her a puzzled look. "Birthstone?"

"You know, in which month was she born?"

Damnation. He didn't know. "I haven't asked."

The woman clapped her hands. "Ooh, it's a new relationship. There's nothing like the first months, right? It's all novel and exciting. What's her favorite color?"

Zut. His annoyance climbed a notch. He should've known little but important things like that.

"I like this one." He pointed at a ring with a center stone surrounded by smaller ones, shaped like a five-pointed star.

"Rubies. Good choice." She removed it from the showcase and handed it to him. "Have a closer look."

The sun caught the color of the stones, illuminating their depths. They were dark and rich, their beauty turbulent. Perfect.

"I'll take this one."

"Shall I giftwrap it for you, sir?"

"Please."

A short while later, he was making his way back to his prisoner.

He was pleased. He'd only made a short detour and delayed his return with a few minutes. The warmth in his chest as he felt the gift in his pocket made every second worthwhile. Presenting Ilse with a gift gave him more pleasure than what she could ever derive from it. He'd never thought giving could feel this good. The closer he got to the mine dumps, the more excited he got. Patience. He had to wait for the right moment. It wouldn't do any good to rush it and spoil the experience. Yes, he'd bide his time. It would prolong the fuzzy feeling he suddenly had in his chest.

NO MATTER how hard she tried, Ilse couldn't sleep. She paced the room, breathing in and out to calm herself and trying hard not think about the fact that she was locked up in a small space. She was walking around the bed for the thousandth time when the wall opened and Drako barged through.

"What is your date of birth?"

She blinked at him. "What?"

"When were you born?" he asked impatiently.

"July third."

"How old are you?"

"Twenty-eight."

"What's your favorite color?"

"Drako, what's going on? Why are you asking all these questions?"

"Answer me."

"Blue."

"Favorite food?"

"Italian."

"Italian?"

"Any pasta dish or pizza."

"What's your favorite drink?"

"Drako, please. You're acting weird. What's the meaning of this line of questioning?"

He closed the distance, stopping short of her. "I'm getting to know you."

Without thinking, she touched his cheek. "Getting to know people takes time."

"We don't have time," he said harshly. "I need to know everything. Now."

"It doesn't work like this," she whispered.

"Why not? I'll ask you questions, and you'll tell me what I want to know."

"Those are not the things that matter. Those facts are superficial. If you really want to get to know someone, you have to spend time together, see how that person behaves, and what makes them tick."

He grabbed her to him so suddenly she cried out with a start.

"Then I'll make the best of the time we have." He pushed the sleeves of the dress over her shoulders. "I'll start with getting to know your body and what makes it tick."

Blood rushed through her veins, making her skin tingle. "I think you've already established that."

"Not by a long shot. There's a million other ways in which to have you." He pushed the dress over her hips and released the clasp of her bra.

Cool air washed over her breasts, contracting her nipples. When his mouth closed around one, she forgot every protest she was going to make, losing herself in a man who hated her as much as he wanted her body.

14

Four Earth weeks had gone. With every passing day, Drako's anxiety grew. Ilse wasn't in a better state. She was listless, her spirits dwindling. Seeing nothing but the walls for days couldn't be good for her. He opened the roof at night, showing her the stars and their constellations, but not even that helped. She made a good job of trying to hide her distress, but there wasn't much about her state of mind or body he missed. The time the Council had granted him was coming to an end, and so was their time together.

When the morning of the day he'd agreed to take her to Kahvissar arrived, he woke her with a long and passionate kiss. As always, she reacted to him immediately, her heartbeat picking up and her pussy growing wet and swollen. The sound of her pulse and the smell of her arousal drove him insane, but he wanted to go slow today.

He moved down her body to taste her nipples, loving how they peaked in his mouth and how she arched her back when he bit down softly. He tested her folds with a finger, even though his sense of smell had already told him she was ready. He was still mindful of not hurting her, keeping in mind how small and fragile she was. They had grown accustomed to each other's bodies, and her actions were confident now as she cupped her hand over his on her sex, showing him what she wanted. He parted her folds with his finger, but didn't penetrate her. Sweet protesting sounds escaped her throat. Mercilessly, he teased her, playing with her clit until she thrashed under him.

"Take me already," she said on a gasp.

"Not today, little doll. Today, I'm taking my time."

He abandoned her breasts to seek out her mouth. Her lips were cool and seductive, her tongue branding him with heat. The contrast was amazing. It did wicked things to his mind, imaging those lips and tongue on his dick.

She broke the kiss, staring at him with her intoxicating blue eyes. "I want to taste you."

Zut, yes. He pushed to his knees, straddling her stomach. She grabbed his hips and pulled him closer, until his cock nudged at her lips. Holding his gaze, she curled her tongue around the crest, dragging a path of fire down the underside to his balls. He clenched his ass, holding onto the last threads of his control. He wanted to give her this, to let her take the lead. She kissed her way back up his cock and folded her lips around him. Opening wide, she took him deep. Watching her take him almost made him lose it, coming down her throat before he'd even been inside her pussy. She moaned as she guided his hips, moving him in and out of the wet heat of her mouth. When he could take no more, he pulled free, inviting another protest.

His turn. He kissed his way down her body to the sweet spot between her legs, taking his time to nibble and lick.

"Drako." She gripped his shoulders. "I want you to bite me."

He lifted his head to look at her. "It's too soon. I'll love you beautifully instead."

No more. He couldn't wait longer. Kneeling between her legs, he parted her folds and pressed home. Her slickness eased his way, her muscles adapted to his size. He wasted no time in burying himself to the hilt. He wanted to be inside her as deep as he could go. After a few shoves, she pushed on his shoulders, indicating she wanted him to stop. He did so only by sheer willpower.

"Turn around," she instructed.

He smiled at the command in her voice. Flipping around onto his back, he brought her with him. Crute. She was a sight to behold on her knees with her thighs spread and his cock buried inside her. As she lifted and lowered her hips, she gave him a prime view of how her pussy stretched to take him. He liked it. Very much. It took everything he had not to slam up and take back control. Gritting his teeth, he let her go at her pace. She moved faster, until sweat covered their bodies and the sound of their pants filled the room. He knew at the exact moment she was going to come. Her face distorted with pleasure a second before her pussy contracted around his cock. Her ecstatic moan was enough to make his tightly coiled control snap. Letting go, he came with violent spams, pouring his seed into her, claiming her as his, even if he knew it would never be.

Falling over him, she rested her head on his chest. He held her to him and rubbed her back, not ready to break their physical or emotional connection. When he couldn't put it off any longer, he kissed the top of her head.

"Go have your shower and get dressed." He moved her gently and stood. "I'll fix breakfast."

Her tone was playful. "I can cook, you know. You don't have to prepare all my meals."

"It's part of the perks of being a prisoner."

He'd said it jokingly, trying to keep the mood light, but her eyes turned somber. Damn him. He was such an idiot.

He touched her cheek. "I didn't mean to…" What? Remind her what she was? Why she was here? His big, infallible master plan had just fallen to pieces. Revenge wasn't sweet, after all. Instead of weaning himself off her, he'd gotten more addicted. "Never mind."

He dropped his hand and stomped from the room before he said more hurtful things.

While Ilse ate, he showered and dressed. She'd cleaned up the kitchen when he walked back into the room.

"I have something for you." He held the gift box from the Bruma Market out to her.

A smile transformed her face into something angelic as she reached for it. "For me?"

"Open it." He held his breath. Would she like it? Would she get the meaning, what he was trying to tell her?

Carefully, she unwrapped the box and lifted the lid. "Oh, my God. Drako, it's beautiful."

"Try it on."

She slipped the ring onto the middle finger of her right hand. The stones shone like bleeding stars. The color stood out against the paleness of her skin. The design emphasized the slenderness of her hand, making her seem even more delicate.

"It suits you."

She splayed her fingers and held her hand up to the light. "I love it. It's gorgeous. But…"

His elation at seeing his gift on her hand faltered. "But what?" Would she refuse to keep it? Maybe she didn't want something to remind her of him. Maybe she wanted to forget.

"But why?" she asked, watching him intently.

It was a symbol of his affection, and a selfish part of him wanted her to remember him, even when she was another Krinar's charl. The elation of presenting her with a gift suddenly turned heavy. Where it was joyful when he'd acquired it, the significance now felt sad.

"If you don't know why, you'll figure it out in time." He held out a hand. "Let's go."

"Where?"

"Home."

"Home?"

"My planet."

"Your planet!" She took a step away. "You're out of your mind."

"At least there you'll be safe. If you stay here, your government will eventually catch you. They're a lot more powerful with more resources than you."

She clutched at the island counter at her back. "I don't want to go to your planet."

"It's not a request, Ilse. You don't get a choice in the matter. Look at it this way, at least you'll be rid of me."

"You're letting me go?"

"Yes." The word sliced right through him. "I'm letting you go."

"I'm free?"

From here. From him. "That's what I said."

She reached for him. "Drako, please don't do this. I don't know your planet. This is my home. This is where I belong."

"No more arguing!"

At his tone, she flinched.

"We're leaving. Now. It's not up for discussion. Either you come willingly or I'll use the necessary force."

"Where exactly are you taking me? To a town? A settlement? Does it have a name? How am I supposed to live there? Will I be able to even breathe in your atmosphere? Where will I live? How will I earn a living?"

So many questions, not enough answers. "You'll see."

She grabbed his arm. "No. This is my life. I have a right to know."

"You have no more rights, little doll, only goodwill, so don't test it." Not able to stand her wounded look, he added in a softer tone, "We'll stop at a space station first. You'll learn all you need to know about Krina there."

Resignation showed in the drop of her shoulders.

He turned his back on her and made his way to the docking bay where the pod was parked.

Ilse squinted at the bright sunlight when they got outside. The way she looked around and dragged the polluted air into her lungs as if it was the first time in her life she came outdoors released a dam of guilt inside him. Pushing it aside, he helped her inside the pod. When he'd secured her safety harness, he took off for the Krina station where Kahvissar was waiting.

"This is unreal," she said, staring down at her planet through the transparent floor as the pod lifted off.

He didn't miss the way her nails dug into the armrests of her chair.

"Don't worry," he said. "You're safe."

"You crashed with a thing like this, didn't you?" she asked in a thin voice.

"It's been upgraded since."

"What if someone sees us? If we can see out, they must be able to see in, right?"

"We're invisible to the outside world." He regarded her pale cheeks. "Are you all right?"

"It's just a bit frightening, the way we're flying as if we're in nothing but a chair, and how fast we seem to move, but it's better than to feel closed into the small space of your plane."

He smiled. We call it a pod," he reminded her.

"Your pod."

He cupped her hand. "You'll be fine."

He wasn't only referring to the flying. Thinking of it made him to want kick objects and tear at the sky. He released her hand.

This way was best.

For both of them.

———

IT WAS like being in a dream. Ilse wasn't sure if it was a good or bad one. She looked around the space station as Drako led her from the parking bay to security and from there to a set of rooms with long windows showing the darkness of space sprinkled with stars and planets. A man taller and bulkier than Drako but with the same yellow eyes and flawless, golden skin came to his feet as they entered a room at the end of the corridor.

Feeling overwhelmed, she wanted to reach for Drako's hand, but he'd been strangely distant since this morning's sex. Instinctively, she knew he wouldn't welcome the contact.

"Bienvenue," the man said, walking to her with outstretched arms.

She gave Drako a bewildered look, but he offered no explanation as the man placed his hands on her shoulders and pressed his cheek to hers. "You are even more lovely in person than in hologram."

"You've seen pictures of me?" She glanced at Drako again.

"But of course."

"This is Kahvissar," Drako said tightlipped. "He offered to take you as charl."

"What?" She slipped from Kahvissar's hold, looking between the men. "What is that supposed to be? Some kind of maid?"

"A maid?" Kahvissar gave a hearty laugh. "It's a life-long companion. A human mate. In Earth terms, I suppose you'd call it a wife."

The world gave way under her feet. If not for Kahvissar's steadying hands, she would've dropped to her knees. Pain lanced at her heart. She searched Drako's eyes, but he simply stood there with a cold expression. Unfeeling.

"Is she unwell?" Kahvissar asked.

"She'll be fine. It was her first space journey."

Pressing a hand on her stomach, she took a shaky breath. It took all her strength to hold back the tears that burned behind her eyes. "Am I a commodity to be passed from one of you to another? Like a pet or possession?"

"Ah, zut." Kahvissar shot Drako a look. "You didn't tell her. You're a first-class troll, Drako."

"It's not safe to let you go back to Earth," Drako said. "Your government will convict you for your crimes, if not assassinate you for the role you played in my escape. You can only be granted access to Krina or one of its settlements as a charl. Kahvissar volunteered for the role."

She backed up to the wall. She felt sick. Shocked. Betrayed. "I see. Is that why you gave me the ring? It's a keepsake?" she asked bitterly.

"It's best like this for both of us," Drako continued. "It's not you, per se. It's that I can never trust you."

"I didn't work for the government agents. It was a ploy to win time to help you escape. Neither did I steal medicine to run a black market operation. Yes, I bought medicine on the black market to help a patient, but as for the rest, I was framed."

Drako's face turned hard. "Ilse, stop. Don't make a fool of yourself. I was *there*. I heard and saw with my own eyes and ears."

It hurt. The coldness in her heart seemed to spread through her whole body until there wasn't a part of her that didn't feel frozen. She'd developed feelings for him, strong ones at that, but if this was truly what he believed of her, he didn't deserve her.

Biting back her tears, she lifted her chin. "Goodbye, Drako."

He nodded once at Kahvissar and then stalked from the room, not looking back.

15

The terrain on the unnamed planet Drako was inspecting for sand kiting was brittle and cold. His den had temperature control and all the comforts that came with one, but he couldn't shake that coldness or the emptiness that pressed on his heart. It was worse than the pain he'd suffered in the hands of the agents on Earth. For that, he only had a pretty little human doll to blame. No matter how hard he tried, he couldn't stop thinking about her. He wasn't going to contact Kahvissar and meddle in their private lives. They deserved undisturbed time together to complete their bonding. Had Kahvissar presented her at Krina? Did Kahvissar enjoy her body as much as he had? He jumped from the plank where he was working and paced to the kitchen. Maybe just a quick call, to see if she'd adapted. No, damnation. He pressed a fist to his mouth. He had to be strong. Kahvissar had warned him about the physical addiction of taking human blood, but he'd failed to mention the emotional addiction would be much stronger.

Damn it. Zut. He activated his palm device, hesitated for all of one second, and called Kahvissar via voice command.

"Drako," his friend replied in a jovial tone. "How's the unknown territory? Still getting a kick out of the adventure?"

He wasn't interested in small talk. "How is Ilse doing?" His heart contracted, the cavity between his ribs filling with bitter poison as he imagined her naked in the arms of his friend. He continued his pacing. "Is she happy? Has she adapted to Krina?"

"I didn't take her to Krina."

Hope flared in his chest. "She's still there, at the station?" Maybe he could catch a glimpse of her.

"She went back to Earth."

He stopped dead. "She did what?"

"She left."

"I heard you fine, you moron. How could she have left?"

"I let her go."

"What do you mean you let her go? She's your charl!"

"No, she's not. She rejected me and asked that I send her home. I had no choice."

"Why?" An ache started throbbing in his temples. "Why would she reject you and risk her life?"

"She said she only cared for you."

He advanced to the hologram in two strides. "Cared for me?"

"She said she loved you."

Drako balled his hands into fists. His voice rose in volume with every word. "You didn't think to check with me before you let her go?"

"You said you didn't want her as charl. Why would I have checked with you?"

"Zut! You're an idiot. You put her life in danger. Do you know what her government will do to her if they catch her, which, right now, is more of a certainty than a probability?"

"Sadly, yes, I understand that they'd eliminate her, which is why I let her go. It serves us, too. This way, she won't talk about the invasion. We can't risk information slipping out before the time is right."

"Zut zut zut!" He rushed to the floating desk, gathering his material.

"Drako, what are you doing? Need I remind you that you have no authorization to go back to Earth?"

"I guess I'll just have to risk the Elders' wrath."

"I insist that you--"

He cut the feed before Kahvissar could utter more protests. Inside his pod, he programmed the coordinates for Earth and set off at maximum speed. He only hoped it wasn't too late.

"I CAN'T MEET with you again, Caitlin." Ilse twisted the ruby ring around her finger. Like always, it sparked bitter-sweet memories she couldn't let go. "It's too risky."

They were in an alley behind a supermarket where they'd agreed to meet. Driving around her house in a rented car had confirmed that it was still being watched. So was the hospital. Caitlin's landline and mobile phone had been tapped, too.

"At least tell me where you're staying," Caitlin said. "I'm going out of my mind with worry about you."

"It's better that you don't know. Did you bring it?"

Caitlin took the Rifampin from her pocket and handed it over. "I can't keep on smuggling medicine out like this. After the allegations, the police are watching the hospital with hawk eyes, searching for any leads to you."

"I'm sorry to put you in this situation. I wouldn't have asked if it wasn't a matter of life and death."

"It's for that patient, the one you promised to visit, isn't it?"

"She's a good woman. She doesn't deserve to suffer because of corruption."

"Tell me what I can do to help you."

"You can stay out of it. The last thing you want is to be implicated."

Caitlin sighed. "You can't call me again as my mother. If someone catches on and compares the numbers, they'll put two and two together."

"You're right." Ilse glanced over her shoulder. "I have to go." She took Caitlin into a hug.

Tears trembled in Caitlin's voice. "You say it like it's goodbye."

She wasn't going to lie to one of the few friends she had. "Take care of yourself. Keep your nose clean and stay out of trouble. Whatever you do, don't get messed up with the medicine scandal. It's not worth it."

Caitlin sniffed. "You, too, honey, and get some sleep. You look like shit."

Ilse smiled. "Thanks, not only for the medicine, but so much more."

The women hugged again briefly.

Ilse left the alley, not looking back at her friend for the fear that she'd break down and cry. It had been a tough month, living from hand to mouth, mostly on Mosa's charity. Thankfully, Samuel was no longer a threat. When the inhabitants of the township had found out what he'd done, they'd beaten him with sticks and expelled him with stones. They didn't take kindly to the betrayal of their own, and Mosa was a respected and loved figure. She held much influence over the informal settlement community.

Mosa was sitting on a box outside the shack when Ilse arrived.

"I have your medicine," Ilse said, handing it over.

"You shouldn't do this," Mosa chastised. "Have you learned nothing?"

Ilse chuckled. "Let you die while those black market bastards make a packet? I don't think so." She sat down next to Mosa on the ground. "I have a plan."

"I don't like it."

Ilse clicked her tongue. "You haven't even heard it, yet."

"I don't care. I don't want to. I know it's going to be bad."

"It's no use stealing and conniving every month to get your

rightful supply of medicine. We need to take down the black market operation and prove my innocence."

She couldn't approach the government and warn them about the pending invasion with a price on her head. The minute she showed her face, Pete and his cronies would pounce and assassinate her. She had to prove her innocence first.

"No judge will set you free. The police own them. You're a government liability now."

"The media can put pressure on the police force."

"The article you leaked didn't work."

"It must've been intercepted by one of the big shot editors. The government owns the newspapers. I need a watchdog media channel, like Carte Blanche."

"Then what? What proof do you have? They can't go around making wild accusations without proof."

"I don't have proof, yet, but I will."

"See? This is the part I don't like."

"I don't have a choice. I can't run forever, and stopping these dealers is the right thing to do. We need less corruption and more damn medicine."

"Ilse." Mosa stilled her with a hand on her arm. "Let's face it. I'm going to die. There's no point in risking your life for me."

"You're not going to die." She added softly, "Besides, there are many others like you."

"You can't save them if you can't save yourself. Get away from here. I beg you. Go to Lesotho."

"When I've taken the black market down."

Mosa sighed. "You're adamant about this."

"Yes."

"If you won't let me persuade you to give up your crazy idea, at least let me help you."

"You're not getting involved. It's too dangerous. If something happens to me, you have to tell the world the truth." She gripped Mosa's hand. "Will you promise me?"

"All right." The older woman straightened with a groan. "When are you doing it?"

"Tomorrow."

"So soon?"

"Not soon enough."

"I'm sorry I took so much of your time."

It had taken Ilse a month to doctor Mosa back to health. The state she'd found her in after not having had access to medicine had left her close to death. Too close.

"It's not your fault." Ilse hugged her. "I'm sorry I wasn't here for you."

"It wasn't your fault, either. If that alien hadn't abducted you--"

"Let's wash up for dinner."

She didn't want to be reminded of the alien who believed the worst of her and traded her like a piece of animal hide.

No, thanks.

It was enough that he dominated her dreams.

At three o'clock in the afternoon, Ilse moved through the Oriental Plaza, trying to blend in with the other shoppers. As agreed, the Carte Blanche crew was positioned around Fatima's Fabrics with hidden cameras. She was wearing one, too, a small device hidden in a pin fitted to her jacket. Tonight, when the broadcast went live, the illegal drug syndicate and the police's involvement would be exposed. Sweat trickled between her shoulder blades. She wore a hat and sunglasses, but the chances were good the dealer would recognize her. Hopefully, he wouldn't call the SS in exchange for the reward on her head.

She made her way through the market buzzing with activity and up the escalators. A man stood in front of the pet shop window, admiring the goldfish. He had to be one of the cameramen. Another stood at the rail, smoking and overlooking the commotion below.

"Hello. Hello," the parrot called in his shrilly voice.

With her heart beating in her throat, she entered the shop. The same woman from her first visit stood behind the counter. The look she gave Ilse was foul.

"Ismael," she called as the door closed behind Ilse. "Your client is back."

The curtain lifted, and the man with the gold-framed spectacles looked around the frame. "A returning customer is always a sign of good service." His smile was broad. "Come on in."

She crossed the doorstep and took a position in front of the desk where the camera would have a good angle on the shelves stocked with medicine.

"The same?" he asked.

"Yes. I'll take two boxes."

"You've got the money?"

"Of course."

She didn't have three thousand rand, but it didn't matter. The minute he handed her the medicine, the charade was over.

While he unlocked the cabinet, she asked in an even tone, "Where does your stock come from?"

"Here and there." He smiled at her from over his shoulder. "I have my regular suppliers."

Staff members at the hospital, no doubt.

"How much do you pay?"

"Why? Are you a supplier?"

"Maybe. I'm a nurse."

"If you're a nurse, why are you here?"

She fiddled with the strap of her handbag. "We're out of stock."

After considering her reply for a moment, he said, "Thanks, but I'm good. If I need something in the future, I'll let you know. You can leave your number."

"Good." She swallowed.

She'd done it. He'd admitted to be willing to buy stolen goods. All that was left was for him to hand over the medicine, and Carte Blanche would have a solid case.

"I only have one box here," he said with his head in the cabinet. He shut the door and locked it. "Let me get another from my stockroom downstairs."

"That's all right," she said quickly. "I'll come back for the other one later."

"It'll only take me a minute," he said with a smile.

Whistling, he left the room. She wrung her hands together. The minutes ticked on. She could almost hear the second hand moving in her mind. Why was he taking so long? Maybe this was a mistake. She was about to step into the shop front when he returned, carrying the Rifampin in his hand. She let out a shaky breath. Thank God. She opened her palm, waiting. He held out the medicine, the smile on his face unfaltering. She closed her eyes briefly. Almost there. As her fingers folded around the box, the curtain flew open. A blur of movement and shouting followed. A bag was thrown over her head. She screamed at the top of her lungs, but it became more difficult to breathe without gagging. The smell inside the terrifying confines of the bag was sharp. Chloroform. Before claustrophobic hysteria could overcome her, darkness scooped down and swept her along.

ILSE'S THROAT ACHED. Her tongue was thick. At first, she thought she was in the den where Drako had taken her. Stupidly, her heart started beating faster in twisted anticipation. Only when she opened her eyes and managed to focus did she realize the cruel trick her hope and memory had played on her. She was in the cell where the SS had kept Drako, chained to the wall, albeit still dressed.

Panic overwhelmed her. She jerked her head toward the

mirror. They were watching. She might as well let them know she was awake. There was no point in prolonging this. As she'd expected, the door opened.

Frik entered with Pete on his heels.

"There's my bitch," Frik said with a sneer. "I knew you'd eventually go back to the black market. All I had to do was wait."

The dealer had betrayed her, after all. He'd probably called in after her first visit, trying to claim the reward.

Frik advanced until he stood in front of her. "You thought you could help that cocksucker alien escape and get away with it? Where is he?"

She fought her nausea, an after-effect of the chloroform. On second thought, maybe she should vomit on Frik's shiny shoes.

"Answer me!" Spit fell from his mouth on her face.

She turned her head sideways. "He made it back to his planet."

"You know this how?"

"He told me."

"He *called* you from space?" he asked mockingly.

She looked back at him with defiance. "Yes."

"Don't you use that cocky attitude with me. You fucking drugged us. What you did is a federal offense, not to mention your *drug trafficking* history."

"You framed me so you could catch me."

His shoulders shook with a cold laugh. "It worked, didn't it?"

"What about the black market? Charge me with whatever crime you think I committed by helping a kidnapped and tortured man you would have allowed to die from his injuries, but do your job. Shut down the black market."

He snickered. "Thanks for the lead. More payback for us."

Her shoulders sagged, making her arms draw tight in the chains.

"That's right, sweet tits. The dealer isn't going down, and we're not laying charges against him."

"You mean you're just going to kill me."

Pete stepped forward. "Unless you tell us where the alien is."

"I already told you, he went back to his planet."

"All we have to do is keep you," Frik said, "and use you as bait. He has the hots for you. He'll come."

"No, he won't."

If he was prepared to give her away like a second-hand piece of furniture, he wasn't going to risk his life to save her. He'd cut all ties after leaving her with Kahvissar. He wouldn't even know she was dead.

She burst into a fit of hysterical laughter, tears of laughter mixing with tears of sadness. Poor Mosa. Without medicine, she'd die. She'd failed her. She'd failed all the other thousands like Mosa. She'd failed her planet. The Krinar would invade Earth and wipe out mankind.

"Drako," she said through dry lips, "he believed I betrayed him. He thinks I worked with you. His leaders are going to issue an order to invade our planet and wipe out the human race. He thinks we're all cruel and deceitful. We have to convince him otherwise. He has to convince his leaders to give us a chance."

Frik laughed again. "Nice try. If you think that bullshit story is going to win you time, you're making a big mistake. Your hourglass ran out the day you tricked us. As it turns out, the motherfucker is infertile. We can't do shit with his sperm. He's a liability to us and so are you. If he's left our hemisphere, our satellites would've picked up a foreign flying object, but it didn't. He's still here, on this planet, hiding somewhere. The minute he crawls out of his hole, you're both dead."

She shot a pleading look at Pete. "He's not coming back. You have to believe me. Help me, or we're all going to die."

"Sorry." Pete shook his head, his expression grave. "We'll give it twenty-four hours. If he doesn't show up, we have no choice but to kill you."

Frik put his nose inches from hers. "It's not going to be quick. No, sweet tits. You can count on it being slow."

THE TRACKER DRAKO had planted on Ilse when he'd healed her pinpointed her current location. The coordinates made him go cold to his core. She was back with her associates, those human filth SS agents. Maybe she was back with her lover, Frik. Maybe that was why she'd risked her life by running from the safety Kahvissar had offered. Maybe she loved Frik.

Maybe. Maybe. Maybe.

Maybe he'd look like a fool, barging back into her life to save her. Maybe he should turn back.

To the seven moons with that. He didn't care that she'd lied, cheated, and deceived her way into his heart. If she regretted what she'd done, even with a tenth of her soul, he was willing to work on his forgiveness. He'd learn to trust her. He'd give her another chance. Wasn't that what love was about?

Yes, damn it. He was going back not only to ensure she was safe, but also to beg her to try with him. They'd shared something beautiful, powerful, fierce. He'd been around for long enough to know that kind of chemistry didn't happen every day. Only once in five hundred Earth years if a Krinar was lucky.

"Course steady," he instructed the pod with renewed resolution.

Kahvissar's face appeared on the communication system screen.

"Accept call."

A hologram appeared in front of him. Kahvissar looked uncharacteristically nervous. "Still heading toward Earth?"

"Yes and no one is going to stop me."

"I explained your situation to the Elders and got you the go-ahead."

"Thank you. That's most considerate."

"Uh, I also followed the signal of Ilse's tracker and hacked into

Earth's satellites to see if I could locate her, and you're not going to like this."

"I know." Drako shifted in his chair. "She's back at her HQ."

"I think she told the truth."

"What?" He moved to the edge of his seat. "What did you see?"

"You better check for yourself."

A feeling of dread made Drako's legs turn to lead. Another image flickered to life next to the hologram, and the recording he saw made him howl in fury.

"Told you it wasn't pretty," Kahvissar said.

"I owe you."

"I'll collect."

Drako cut the hologram of Kahvissar, but kept the other feed alive. It came from a sat that belonged to an Earth news station. The longer he watched, the more infuriated he became, until his vision was a maelstrom of sizzling black. He'd kill those bastards.

Landing on the roof of the old SS building, he made his way through the warehouse that once housed the wreck of his pod, now empty. He easily deactivated their alarms as he went by using his palm device. He charged down the stairs, expecting to see a small army, but instead a big one met him. The humans came well prepared. Before they had time to react, he released the gas from the special pocket of his flight suit. In a nanosecond, they were flat on their backs on the ground, snoring.

He flung back the deadbolt and kicked the door open. At the sight of Ilse hanging in the very chains that had once detained him, his body went colder than the seven moons. His fury spiked. His vision turned dark. He took in everything in a flash. Frik had a weapon trained on Ilse, and Pete was standing a short distance behind him, a gun in his holster. The immediate danger was Frik. The agent's eyes turned big as his defective, rotten brain took in Drako's speedy entrance. He swung the gun in Drako's direction, but Drako was faster than the human's trigger finger. Before Frik could react, Drako grabbed his arm and flung him through the air.

He hit the wall like a fly. His motionless body lay on the floor, the gun bent and useless.

"Drako!"

That voice, the most beautiful one he'd ever heard, called out to him in distress. He swung around to face her, ready to defend, to kill any man who laid his hands on her. What he saw made him tremble with rage. Pete had his pistol pressed to her temple, his finger trembling on the trigger.

"Let me go," the agent said, "or she dies."

Drako laughed. "Where are you going to go?" He advanced slowly. "There's nowhere I won't find you."

The barrel of the gun shook even more. "Stop. If you come any closer, I'll shoot her, I swear."

Drako paid the man no heed. All he could focus on was the gun against his fragile human's head. He was acutely aware of her mortality. If anything happened to her, his life would be empty, an endless stretch of pain and torture. Close enough now to reach for the gun, he lifted his arm. At the speed he was moving, Pete would hardly have time to notice, never mind to pull the trigger, but the agent surprised him. He had to have anticipated the move. As Drako grabbed his wrist and forced his arm down, the shot went off.

The horrid sound echoed in Drako's skull. The stench of gunpowder filled the room with its potent, damaging smell. A red stain blossomed on Ilse's side. Drako froze in shock, his fingers still clamped around Pete's wrist, the gun now pointing at the floor. He didn't realize how hard he was squeezing until Pete's scream wiped out the faint vibrations of the gunshot, followed by the sound of bones cracking. Pete fell to his knees, howling like a dog.

Drako let go of his wrist. "The key," Drako hissed, grabbing the man's face in his hand and applying enough force to crack his jaw.

"There's a control," Ilse said in a weak voice, her pain palpable, "in the room." With much effort, she motioned with her head at the one-way mirror.

Too far. He wasn't leaving her sight. "The key," he repeated, shaking Pete like a rag.

"In my pocket," Pete said through sobs and snot.

Drako's heart beat sluggishly in his chest as he searched the agent. He felt every thud like a hammer swinging between his ribs, the smell of Ilse's blood strong in his nose. The dip of the energy as the life force drained from her rendered him weak. His fingers were steady on the key as he finally extracted it from Pete's jacket, but his gut trembled. He made quick work of unlocking her. Her body sagged when the last shackle came free. He grabbed her around the waist, holding her tightly to him.

"Hold on, little doll," he whispered in her hair. "Hold on for me."

"Drako." A faint smile played on her pale face as he lowered her to the floor. "You came."

It was hard to speak through the restriction in his throat. "Of course, I did." He laid her down as gently as he could, reaching for the nano-healer in his utility vest pocket. "Stay with me, do you hear me? Don't close your eyes."

She fought to comply, but her lashes were already fluttering. "How did you find me? Wait." She uttered a pained whimper. "Don't tell me." Her smile turned even fainter. "Technology."

"I planted a tracker under your skin when I healed you. I'm not risking losing you. Ever."

Her eyes fluttered closed.

"Don't black out, darling, not without giving me a chance to tell you why I came back."

He activated the healer and dragged it over her side. She groaned with pain, her cheeks growing paler, but that ghost of a smile didn't leave her lips.

"Tell me," she said, her voice unnaturally soft. "Tell me why you came back."

"I believe I'm addicted to you."

Her laugh ended up in a cough. "You're back for more blood, huh?"

"I was referring to the emotional kind of addiction." He studied his work. The bullet had been pulled out. The wound was closing up and the damaged tissue repairing.

She stared at him with her big, beautiful eyes. "Emotional addiction?"

His body filled with a heat that could only be attributed to utter and complete happiness. "I believe emotional addiction equals love."

"You love me?"

"That's why I gave you a ring." The fact that she was wearing it gave him hope. "You figured it out, didn't you?" The healer had done its job, though she'd still be weak from shock and blood loss. "I know telling you isn't enough. I was hoping you'd give me another chance to show you how sincere my emotions are. It would take time, of course. A very long time. That's what you said, remember?"

"How long exactly?"

"More or less forever."

"I see."

"I know it's asking a lot, but I was hoping you'd forgive me and maybe learn to love me, even if just a little."

"No biting?"

"Oh, I'm going to bite you. You can count on that."

"I was hoping you'd say that."

He picked her up, cradling her body to his chest. "Let's get out of here."

"Yes." She buried her face in his neck. "Take me home, Drako."

EPILOGUE

Hand-in-hand, Ilse and Drako strolled through the dirt roads of Alexandra. He squeezed her fingers tighter, mindful of his strength. He could never get enough of touching her, his human partner. Looking at the way the sun caught the golden color of her hair and the pearly shine of her skin, he was not only reminded of the external beauty that reflected the pureness of her heart, but also of how easily he could've lost her, in more than one way. As his charl, she'd been granted eternal life. He needn't worry about her dying from old age, but that didn't mean she couldn't be injured. The urge to wrap her up in protective microscopic fiber and hide her from the dangers of the universe was still there, but he'd learned to let her soar, to give her the freedom to be the person she was meant to be, the one he'd always love. She'd accepted being his charl, and she'd accepted marrying him. He wanted to tie her to him by all standards––his, hers, in affection, in bed, and in blood. He'd marked her in every way possible to show the world she was his.

"There it is." She pointed at a white building with the word *clinic* painted in red on the wall. "What do you think?"

He smiled down at her. "It's perfect." Like her. Like everything she did.

Ilse had gotten private funding to start a free clinic in the township where a team of volunteer nurses and doctors worked around the clock. The Elders had not yet agreed to make their technology available to Earth. It was too soon. If they'd do so in the future depended on human comportment and how it would unfold. As with all intelligent species, Earthlings had their share of good and bad. Just like the Krinar. He knew that now. For all the bad, there was plenty of good, starting with the woman walking beside him.

He'd amended his recommendation regarding Earth, advising the Elders that cohabitation was not only possible, but also desirable. The Council had held their meeting a Krina month ago. Their decision had been made. The invasion would continue with a slow rollout phase of secluded Krinar settlements. Krinar and humans would live side by side. In time, he was certain humans would benefit from Krinar technology. From what he'd seen since he'd been living on Earth with Ilse, he had new faith in them. As for his history on Earth, the Elders had decided to keep it quiet for the sake of universal peace. As far as history went, his was the untold story.

Pete and Frik had been detained, their memories wiped. They now worked as caretakers in a Hospice facility for HIV patients. The medicine black market had been brought down and corruption in the hospitals uprooted. The footage of his rescue of Ilse had been destroyed, leaving Carte Blanche only with enough evidence to clamp down on the black market dealer and his associates. Corruption in government still existed, but like his little human had taught him, Rome wasn't built in a day.

These days, they lived in a dwelling in Costa Rica with a few other Krinar and charls, but they visited Johannesburg on a weekly basis for Ilse to continue with her charity work. His chest swelled with pride whenever he introduced her as his charl. His human mate. For life. When he'd first taken her, he hadn't given her a choice. Not really. These days, in the privacy of their home, she came to him naked, no negotiation required.

Mosa exited the clinic. She wore a white uniform like the other volunteers. "At last." She propped her hands on her hips and smiled. "I thought your honeymoon was delaying you indefinitely. How was Costa Rica?"

"Wonderful." Ilse beamed. "You should come."

"With all this work?" She wiped a hand over her brow. "I won't fit in a visit before Christmas."

For all she scoffed and complained, Drako could see how fulfilling the work was for her. There was a new purpose in her step and a shine in her eyes. He studied her closer. Her coloration looked healthier, too. The Krinar medicine he'd provided had cured Mosa's tuberculosis. It was a special exception granted by the Elders, knowing how much she meant to Ilse.

"Actually," Ilse said, glancing at him, "we were more thinking along definite terms."

"You mean move in with you?" Mosa squinted at them.

"Wouldn't you like that?" Ilse asked, her voice uncertain.

"The two of you aren't too bad," Mosa waved between them, "but I've got my work cut out for me, here. Besides, I haven't had time to enjoy my new house, yet."

Ilse had signed over the deed of her house to Mosa now that she lived in his dwelling.

"Don't fret," Mosa said. "Caitlin told me she was planning a holiday in Costa Rica in December. Maybe we could all meet up for Christmas and spend the month together."

Ilse squealed. "That will be wonderful." She looked at him quickly. "Wouldn't it?"

"Of course." There was nothing he'd deny her. He thanked the stars every day that his mission had sent him to Earth.

"Come," Ilse said, tugging on his hand, "let me give you the tour. We made new improvements to the rehabilitation center."

As Mosa walked ahead of them, he held Ilse back. She paused to look at him with those mesmerizing eyes. Her smell wrapped around him like a caress, instantly waking his appetite. Wrapping his arms around her waist, he pulled her close for a quick kiss, until her smell changed from appetizing to downright edible as her arousal spiked. The kiss lasted much longer than he'd intended, so much so that they were both breathless when he finally let her go.

She gave him a shy smile. "We better go. Mosa's waiting for us."

"Fine, but only if we leave straight after." He tested the next words on his tongue, still feeling the novelty of them as he said, "I want to *make love to you.*"

Her face lit up like a thousand stars. "All you have to do is ask."

Aye. He'd be asking. For the rest of forever.

~ THE END ~

ACKNOWLEDGMENTS

A big, heart-felt thank you to Anna Zaires for opening her **Krinar World** to fans like me, and for allowing new characters on her Krinar stage. All credit for the technology and physical attributes of the Krinar race used in this story goes to Anna Zaires and Dima Zales, with special reference to advanced nanotechnology for healing, transport via pods, Krinar dwellings and their unique characteristics, as well as mention of the coming Krinar Earth Invasion. The Krinar books remain at the top of my favorite futuristic romances, and it was an honor and pleasure to play in this world.

Thank you, Anna and Dima!

Made in the USA
Columbia, SC
28 August 2023

22203892R00100